Bernice Rubens was born in Wales and later read English at the University of Wales, of which she is now a Fellow.

Her writing career began when she was thirty and around the same time she started work in the film industry. For some time, Bernice alternated between writing novels and making films. For the last ten years she has concentrated solely on writing. Her novels to date include the Booker Prize Winner *The Elected Member* and *Five Year Sentence* which was shortlisted for the Booker Prize. In 1987, Bernice was on the Booker Prize jury and she has also won the Welsh City Council Prize for *Our Father*. Two of her books have been successfully transferred to film; *I Sent A Letter To My Love* and most recently *Madame Sousatzka*, directed by John Schlesinger and starring Shirley Maclaine. *Kingdom Come* is her latest novel.

Bernice's other love, apart from writing, is playing the cello. She has two daughters.

Also by Bernice Rubens in Abacus:

BIRDS OF PASSAGE
BROTHERS
THE ELECTED MEMBER
A FIVE YEAR SENTENCE
I SENT A LETTER TO MY LOVE
MADAME SOUSATZKA
MATE IN THREE
MR WAKEFIELD'S CRUSADE
OUR FATHER
THE PONSONBY POST
SPRING SONATA
SUNDAY BEST
GO TELL THE LEMMING
KINGDOM COME

SET ON EDGE

Bernice Rubens

AN ABACUS BOOK

First published in Great Britain by Eyre & Spottiswoode (Publishers) Ltd 1960
Published by Hamish Hamilton Ltd 1987
Published in Abacus by Sphere Books Ltd 1989
Reprinted 1991

Printed in England by Clays Ltd, St Ives plc

ISBN 0 349 10106 X

Sphere Books Ltd
A Division of
Macdonald & Co (Publishers) Ltd
165 Great Dover Street, London SE1 4YA
A member of Maxwell Macmillan Publishing Corporation

To the Memory of my Father

The fathers have eaten sour grapes and the children's teeth are set on edge.

EZEKIEL. 18.2

PART I

1 The trouble with family relationships is conscience, which is nearly always guilty. The Sperber family were guilt-riddled, and as no man will bear his guilt alone but looks for its source, finding there someone to blame or hold responsible, so the Sperbers sought out their rotten root. Each of them knew from the beginning where their search would lead them, and each was afraid of showing the other the way.

But it was sufficient that this lagging search should occupy the most part of their lives, and their interest was maintained by the various detours they made on the way. If one of the Sperbers lost his wallet, he would look in every pocket except the one in which the wallet was kept. If this search failed, he would look in the drawers, among his papers, in his cases; he would turn the house out for his wallet, knowing all the time that there was little possibility of finding it. But never, never would he look in his wallet pocket. He knew that if it wasn't there, then he had definitely lost it, and he would resign himself to its disappearance rather than know irrevocably that it was gone. So the Sperbers safely measured out their days in the sidetracks, the lanes, the by-passes, the diversions, and the thought of finding anything relevant to the object of their search filled them with horror.

It was significant that their way of life, or rather their detour of life, did not change when Mr Sperber died.

The first of Mrs Sperber's brood was Gladys. Gladys Sperber. When people are a legend, they become initialized, disembodied, for they no longer represent a heart that beats. The letters, G.S., by which Gladys came to be called, covered the narrow limitless range of human unhappiness. If someone said you were like G.S., or threatened to become like her, it was saying plenty.

Mrs Sperber was only seventeen when Gladys was born. She knew nothing of the process of childbirth and was well on in her seventh month before she understood her condition. Mrs Sperber was a woman of strict routine. Every day of her week had its appointed task and she knew that her baby would arrive only when her household duties were done and she would have a little time. She had been feeling unwell for a few days, but having miscalculated her time, she refused to ascribe the pains to her condition and carried on normally. It was while she was haggling over a pound of cod in the local market that the first pains of labour visited her. The pain had somewhat numbed her bargaining powers and it took a little longer than usual to beat the fishmonger down to what she considered a fair price. She was still some distance from home, but it was Friday and the Sabbath shopping had to be done. The pains were getting worse. "It's an ill omen," she thought, "that fish man gave me the evil eye." She felt inside her bodice to make sure she hadn't forgotten the little sack of salt she carried around her neck to ward off the evil spirits. It was still there, though perhaps, she thought, a little lighter in weight. Its presence reassured her, and despite the pain, she trudged on from stall to stall, sampling, haggling, buying, until her shopping was complete. In one hand she carried her shopping bag and with the other she clutched the salt-sack round her neck. From the city bridge she could see her home and the forty-five stone steps that led towards it on the waterfront. She looked over the bridge into the water and as the pains tore through her, she pierced the little bag of salt with her finger-nail and felt a slow and steady trickle between her breasts. She thought of the eggtimer that Abel had given her when they were married. "It's got a figure exactly like yours," he said, and she knew her time had come.

She had just reached the gate of her house when the birth-pang assailed her. It was at a quarter past two on a winter Friday, two hours before the first star would announce the arrival of the Sabbath, that her first born dropped inconsiderately and shamelessly on to the door mat. Thus Gladys Sperber fell immediately into her element. The mat was her cradle and, ever afterwards, the womb to which she always returned.

Mrs Sperber re-filled the little salt-sack, and wedged it firmly between the two centre whalebones of her bodice, so that no more children would be born until Gladys was at least old enough to give her a hand. Which was when Gladys was pushing five. Thereafter four other children followed in quick succession.

There was Miriam, Brina, Benny and Sol. And Gladys brought them all up. When Mrs Sperber was too busy in the tailoring shop upstairs, it was Gladys who saw to all

12

the needs of the children. She waited on them; she waited for them. " I'll see to myself when the others are seen to," she would say. She would take her food when the others had eaten. She would wait for the others to fall asleep before she would go to her bed. She would wait for their happiness before she felt entitled to her own, and she would have looked after their dying if she'd been able. From the beginning, she was taken for granted by all the members of her family, and although she complained, she would not have had it otherwise. Most causes find their own martyrs, but Gladys was a martyr *per se*. She waited as each of them, Benny, Sol, Brina and Miriam shed themselves of her, and she was left, waiting, heart-lazy, for nothing.

2 Mrs Sperber's children, each in their own way, were failures. After several abortive attempts at careers, the girls were married, or, for the most part, married off, and the two boys had gone into business. " Buy and Sell ", was their creed. " If you buy and sell ", their father had told them, " you'll make a million." But there must have been quicker ways. Benny, the youngest, had been buying and selling in one way or another for the better part of his forty lean years. As a child he heard it called barter and exchange, but these were adult refinements, and Benny knew when he manipulated a swap of his warped, nibbled ruler for a fountain pen, that this was indeed buying and selling. The one ruler was later replaced by " stock ". To buy stock

was to buy wholesale and to buy wholesale entitled you to wear long trousers and sport a shaving-brush, and before Benny was out of school, he was buying, as he arrogantly told his friends, "in bulk". Bulks of books, bulks of lace, bulks of safety-pins, so long as it was bulk, Benny didn't care, and the books, lace and pins after twenty years still lay in Benny's attic with all the other misbuys Benny had bought wholesale. "One day," he would tell his wife, "there'll be a demand. Mark my words." "Books get older and soon they'll be old enough to be antiques. They'll be worth a mint one day," he told Sadie. He did the same with his safety-pins. "They'll be worth their weight in gold", was the phrase he reserved for his stock of pins. He was less optimistic about the lace. There was too much of it and Sadie, bless her, given a hundred years, and with her passion for pretty clothes, couldn't get through a thousands yards of stock. They would of course make pretty wedding-dresses for his two daughters. Miriam was all right, she'd have no trouble. But Caroline—she wouldn't be so easy. Seven yards set aside and rotting away. Out of the thousand yards that daily gathered dust in its filigree, all could be disposed of, but seven yards had to be kept back for Caroline. Benny no longer worried about the rest. He saw every inch of his lace profitably put to use. He'd paid next to nothing for it anyway. He saw Miriam as a bride absolutely smothered in lace. He could even have a few lace shirts himself, they could use lace dusters, lace curtains, lace bed-spreads, lace sheets—well, maybe not—they could do almost anything with the lace except eat it, and somehow or other he would dispose of the bulk of his bulk. But for seven yards. And he saw his eldest daughter, Caroline, whom he loved more than anyone else in the world, follow him through the remainder of his years, clutching the miserable seven yards to her flat, wretched chest, her bankrupt inheritance. At times a terrible thought struck him. They could be used for a shroud and in a flood of overwhelming love and pity, he no longer wept for his lace, but for Caroline.

And after thirty years in business, Benny still bought and sold. They still only lived in a semi-detached house; he still had to think before using the telephone; wine was drunk only on Festivals, and going to the cinema was still considered a splash. The million his father had promised him was still a long way off. But the compelling phrase, "buy and sell", never lost its magic ring. It was the shibboleth to casinos, rivieras, and smart hotels. Without it, there would only be amusement arcades, Southend and a boarding-house. "Buy and Sell", that's what Father had said. He would repeat this to himself, whenever things looked bad.

Now the part of Benny which did the buying, was of gigantic dimensions, but that which sold, was a dwarf by comparison. He would enter a wholesale house and buy an immeasurable quantity of goods with the air of a potentate, towering over his supplier, donating here and there a magnanimous gesture, his assumed wealth instilling fear and respect in all who served him. His stature would increase as the deal progressed. But selling was a different matter. He would enter the office of a potential customer, nay, he would creep, softly, lest he disturb, he would beg an audience, he would flatter, cajole, humble himself, "you are good to spare me a moment, I know how terribly busy you are, but I'm sure I have just the thing you want, perhaps you'd be interested in three thousand yards of sacking? . . ." Why the hell should he be interested, what in God's name could anyone use three thousand yards of sacking for except curtains, dusters, sheets, wedding-dresses? . . . "But of course I understand, there isn't a market —that crook brother of mine swore by his life there was a market—but you know best. Ah well, perhaps another time, I'll see myself out, thank you, don't bother, thank you," and he diminished with each word until by the time he had reached the door all that could be seen was a tiny dot, overburdened by a huge round sack of sacking, like an inverted doughnut.

When he was home in his family circle, Benny's attitude was conditioned by what he had last done during the day. If he returned home straight from a buying spree, he tended to be gentle, docile even, modest to the point of self-derogation towards Sadie and his two daughters. He felt no doubt he could afford to relax his powers of self-assertion when these were not called for. If, on the other hand, an unco-operative customer had been his last encounter, Benny would return home in a mood of anger, arrogance and conceit, by way of compensation. So Sadie never had to ask how the day had been, dear. After fifteen years of marriage, she was well acquainted with the barometer of his moods. In any case, they suited her. Outside her home and family, she was a woman with no interests, and the necessity of something to fight, of something to envy, a butt for her bitterness, was always with her. If Benny was in a gentle mood, she would hint at his lack of manliness, if arrogant, she would sneer contemptuously at his failure in business. And though both reactions, calculated to provoke, hurt him deeply, he assumed an indifference towards them, for they had both, long ago, exhausted their love for each other. Sadie was the unhappier of the two, but bitterness and unhappiness had never really controlled her. If anyone would even hint to Sadie that all was not well with her, she would tremble with rage at what she considered an intrusion into her private life. If people thought she was unhappy they would presume her marriage was a failure. That was what Sadie wanted least. To fail in marriage was not respectable. There was always a dubious cause. If only to spite Benny's mother, Sadie was determined that her marriage would not break down.

Mrs Sperber had been against it from the start. Benny was her last child, and the love she had been unable to give her other children, because of her fight against motherhood, accumulated and fell to Benny. When Benny was born, she had at last reconciled herself to the fact that, with five children to her credit, she could graciously accept the status of mother. Benny's inheritance of mother-love, was thus entirely disproportionate, and the more she loved him, the greater grew his guilt and the smaller grew the possibility of repayment. It was inevitable, therefore, that as he grew up, Benny talked himself out of this imposed obligation, to the extent that not only would he not repay her, he would rob and cheat her into the bargain. "My blue eye," she would call him. "My Benny'll keep us all. He's going to be a doctor," she would tell her friends. There was no evidence of this but it sufficed that this was Mrs Sperber's decision. "He'll be loved and respected. He'll be a scholar. He'll marry a rich girl from a good Jewish family." This would be the height of his career. Even in Mrs Sperber's eyes there was little else he could achieve. But the nearest Benny ever got to the field of medicine was in his very early infancy, when he was in no position to retreat even on religious grounds. He had never made more money than was necessary to meet his most immediate needs, and to cap it all, he had married Sadie. When he had broken the news of his engagement to his mother, the rest of the family had immediately allied themselves with her. It was guilt, a vicarious guilt, rather than love or loyalty that had prompted their choice. Benny's marriage would have meant vicarious atonement too, it would, by way of compensation, have limited their own choice. No, they had all coddled Benny too long. Now he could stand alone. It was Gladys who attacked first.

"How can you do it to your mother?" she screamed at him. "Didn't I sacrifice everything for you? Didn't I bring you up to be decent? D'you think I couldn't have married fifty times? But no, I've got to stay here and look after Benny. Wait till Benny grows up and marries a decent girl, I said to myself. And what have you done? A no-good you've picked up. What did I sacrifice my life for? So that you should come home with a—a——, well even a shicksa would be better. A fine thanks for all I've done for you!"

"Anyone would think you were my mother," said Benny, trying to divert the course of the argument.

"Well haven't I been a mother to you?" Gladys shouted.

The question rang out like a challenge, and, adjusting her cross, Gladys sank exhausted in the big armchair. It was not Benny, but Mrs Sperber who took upon herself to answer the question.

"What difference does it make? He's my son, isn't he? No one asked you to bring him up, Gladys, no one asked you to sacrifice yourself for my Benny. Don't go blaming people that you're not married. No one's good enough for you. That's your trouble." For a moment Gladys looked at the rest of the family, challenging them to deny their mother's accusation. But everyone was silent, and Gladys, now fully satisfied that nobody loved or needed her, purred gently into her chair, "That's gratitude for you."

Benny was grateful for the respite and patiently waited for his mother and Gladys to decide who had sacrificed what, how much, when and for whom. When Mrs Sperber had dispossessed Gladys of all her claims, she turned her attention to the business in hand. She did not look at Benny as she spoke, but instead turned her wrath on her whole family. She threatened heart-attacks, she threatened suicide—she'd overstepped herself, she knew. She'd come to her end too quickly. Let him suffer a while. Under protest from the rest of the family, she withdrew the suicide proposal and reverted to heart-attacks and, later on, lunacy. These were maladies, she knew, that were not necessarily fatal. Let him for the rest of his life witness her slow decay and know that he was responsible. Benny remained unmoved. His mother's attitude had made him more determined. "Sadie's a wonderful girl," he announced to the family, but the remark was irrelevant. She may well have been a wonderful girl. The point was, she wasn't a rich girl, she had had no education, her father was a taxi-driver, and she came from London. In those days and in a small provincial family, London had only two connotations—Buckingham Palace and Soho. To Mrs Sperber, if you weren't the queen, you were a girl on the streets. There was nothing in between. And when Sadie arrived for the family viewing with her hennaed hair, black fishnet stockings and a rosebud of a mouth, Mrs Sperber knew that the House of Windsor was not in her blood and she dreaded to think what was. And for the first time she sensed defeat. But with her reputation of surmounting all difficulties and overcoming all sorrows, she was not going to fail her public on this account. She turned the short-comings of the situation to her advantage, so much so, that at the wedding she hovered among her guests and was heard to remark several times that of course her sons were not out for money, that Sadie was a poor honest girl, that she, Mrs Sperber, had paid for the wedding herself, and that all that mattered was that they were happy, etcetera. But as she came home that night from the festivities, alone in the joyful company of her family, she thought of Sol, her other son. Maybe

Sol, there's still a chance he'll marry a rich girl from a good Jewish family, but the thought carried little conviction. And anyhow, rich girls were for her Benny. Sol would get no more than he deserved and in Mrs Sperber's eyes, this was very little.

3 Mr Sperber had always wished for a boy, but Emma had stubbornly year after year given birth to girls, until, after a run of three, he suspected her of doing it on purpose. So when Sol was born, he was assumed a misconception and from his birth the whole family regarded him as a stranger. Since his childhood, he had fought and lived alone, creating his own standards as they conformed to his requirements. As his requirements grew, so he adjusted his standards, and when he stole or lied or cheated, it was none of these things, but purely a case of faulty adjustment.

Sol was the disgrace of the family, and when visitors came, delicate arrangements had to be made to keep Sol out of the way. Because Sol had bad manners, he swore, he wore his poverty openly and unashamedly. And since he was alone all the time, creating among the guttersnipes of the neighbourhood a private existence, he did not know that privacy was you in a room with no one else, so he would pick his nose and scratch his arse. He would even break wind, and would make no attempt to cover up the noise by moving a chair or scraping his heel on the floor to demonstrate that this kind of noise could be made by any decent person and quite voluntarily. No, it was impossible to put Sol on show. He was ugly too, and his face bore an uncomfortable family resemblance, though it was difficult to pinpoint the similarity. It seemed that his face had been endowed with all the left-overs. Whereas the rest of the family had features that belonged to each other, everything Sol had didn't match. His face looked as if it had come in on the last day of the sales, and had out of sheer necessity to take what was going. Even the two ears were not exactly alike either in size or shape; his face was a composite of oddments and seconds, and though he had managed to get everything there was no ensemble.

When he was sixteen, he joined the army. "He's not even conscripted," Mrs Sperber moaned, "he's volunteered." To volunteer for anything, in Mrs Sperber's eyes, was an act of lunacy. "You've publicly disgraced the family," she accused. "My son, in the army! Well," she quickly seized the advantage, "it may knock some sense into you." But all the army knocked into Sol was three large pieces of shrapnel, and an even stronger conviction, when he was invalided out, that the world owed him a living.

When they had brought him into the field hospital, his heavy listless body, relaxed by pain, gave the appearance of a corpse, and in the chaos of the moment, when only a cursory examination was possible, he was shunted on his wagon along the convoy of "stiffs" to the hospital morgue, where he lay a whole night in almost as deep a sleep as his bed-fellows. When he awoke, writhing with the pain of his wounds, he sensed the darkness and feared that his sight was impaired. He struggled to decipher a shape in the darkness or some object he could identify but there was only blackness and a terrible unearthly smell. He suddenly remembered a blind boy he had known in his youth, whose sense of smell was uncannily acute. "I'm blind," he convinced himself, "I'm blind," he shouted, savagely wiping the hot tears from his face. "O God," he sobbed, "O God, please God, I'll be good, but let me see, let me see. I'll use my eyes, I will, all my life. I'll never shut them again, I promise, please God." He unfolded his hands and let them squint slantwise to the sides of his body. His fingers licked the cold slab of his bed, and he thought it was fear that so chilled him. He raised his body slowly and dropped his legs to the floor. He didn't trust his balance, so he sat for a while on the cold slab. He turned his head slowly and discerned a chink of morning light through the half-closed shutters of the window. "I've got striped eyes," he thought, "like a prisoner who has spent years looking at his bars." This thought occurred to him even before he realized he could see at all. He was tempted to thank God for the miracle, but he realized that he had only thought he was blind and thus he was under no obligation to be grateful. The contempt he felt for himself for having momentarily succumbed to faith, he quickly transferred to the faith itself and he swore aloud. He sat on his slab for a while longer, and as his eyes grew accustomed to the dim light, he slowly discerned the figure and faces of his companions. "How silently they all sleep," he thought, and once again fear filled him.

He tentatively tested his feet and the desperation of pain and fear strengthened him so that he was able to lurch to the neighbouring slab. He stared into the face of his bed-mate and felt the decay of his flesh. But whose face, and whose flesh, whether his own or his companion's, he was too confused to understand. The eyes were staring severely as if to apologize for the obscene grin Death had left stamped on the rest of the face. He looked round frantically, and lurched towards one slab and yet another. And always the same stare, the hideous smile and the rank foetid smell of decay. "O God," he murmured, "please, please God, don't let me be dead. I promise, I——" and inwardly he cursed himself for his former ingratitude, "I promise I'll use every minute of my life, I'll serve you. I promise, I promise. I don't want to be dead," he thundered. "D'you hear me, God damn you, I don't want to be dead. I'm dead," he whimpered, "I'm dead," and slowly, his strength leaving him, he crawled on his belly to the door of his earthly tomb. "I'm dead," he cried into the crack. "Bury me, alone, alone, in the dark, where I can lie in peace."

For the last five minutes, the morgue official had been sitting in his office outside the morgue, and once or twice, he thought he had heard strange noises coming from inside. His was a profession which either nurtured the imagination to uncontrollable dimensions, or else atrophied it completely. On this official in particular the profession had had the former effect. Fear had seized him too, which was why some time had elapsed before he could bring himself to investigate. But he

lacked courage and was obliged to call his two assistants to witness what they would find. The door seemed
reluctant to open and as it gave way, it pushed back
the body of sobbing Sol, and the three officials stood
there, transfixed, listening to the plaintive voice beg-
ging for a decent burial. When his fear had found its
cause, the morgue official felt extreme annoyance. The
situation cast undoubted reflection on his efficiency.
"But you were dead yesterday," he accused. "Yes, I'm
dead," Sol whispered, "good and dead." He was not
sure what the morgue official represented. The main
thing was that he was vertical, and with his white coat
and bunch of jangling keys, he looked as if he could
do something for him. With his last ounce of strength,
Sol crawled towards his feet, confirming his corpse-
status to the official's shoe-lace. Then the pain was no
longer bearable and he fell unconscious.

In the year that Sol spent in hospital, among his own
family he was regarded with respect, and though he was
still a stranger to them, wounded and common soldier
that he was, he was a stranger of whom they were
secretly proud. Mrs Sperber concluded that Sol's contribution to the war effort was big enough to be considered
as on behalf of the whole family. She was now in a
position to afford patriotism, since Benny was too young
at the time and she even taunted other mothers who
had not partially sacrificed their sons. In the year that
Sol lay in hospital, she visited him regularly, she and
Gladys, each time taking him some delicacy she knew
would please him, enough for himself, for his nurses,
and for those who lay by his side. And as long as he was

on the danger list, she loved him, she cared for him, and with her tit-bits, she won friends for him. When after a year he left hospital, his arms and legs permanently mangled with scars, he, at least, of all the members of the Sperber family, bore a visible wound, an outward receipt to his mother of a partial pay-off.

The war was over. The joy at reunion and the gratitude for survival degenerated into tedium and indifference. The old hatreds were renewed and families resumed their private warfare after the period of truce. The Sperber tensions were re-strung and the household went back to normal. Sol loafed around for a few years, always willing to earn money in any way as long as it wasn't legal, and in this way he stacked a small fortune. He was generous. People who disliked him ascribed his generosity to a means of making friends; but whatever its purpose, it was wholehearted and extreme. He was never short of women, but no affair lasted very long. To Sol, a woman was a deal like any other; there was no time for patter or preliminaries. The results of his sudden enthusiasms cost his father much in hush money to uphold the family name. So everyone was relieved when Sol took up with Lily. When the liaison had lasted a fortnight, which in Sol's case was an eternity, Mrs Sperber hastened to make arrangements for the marriage. The local Rabbi was summoned to perform the rites and thus Sol participated in his first experience that was sanctioned by the law. With what seemed astonishing speed, Lily gave birth to a daughter, and a year later, they had a son. And both children grew up in the image of their father.

4 Miriam was obviously a throw-back. Although she had her mother's beauty and Mr Sperber's gentleness, she had something they both lacked. She was perceptive, rational, she was the nearest approach to an intellectual in the whole family. When she was three, she was reading, and at four, writing letters to herself, the contents of which she would put completely out of her mind until she received them; then she would reply immediately, answering the questions she had posed herself and always leaving a loophole for further argument. This mirror-correspondence continued throughout her 'teens, so that by the time she was eighteen, she knew herself pretty well. Her brothers and sisters realized that she was of a different cut and when she passed her teachers' examinations and became a leader of the local suffragettes, they feared and respected her. Even Gladys, who had come to regard herself as indispensable, gave way to Miriam when a decision had to be made. Of her weekly wage, Miriam gave half to the suffragettes and half to Mrs Sperber, who could never understand why her portion was no bigger, but even she was too intimidated by Miriam to argue her rights.

War had broken out and Mr Sperber had earned a Government contract for officers' uniforms. The Sperbers were never to see better days. But Sol's room was empty. The lunatic had gone to the war. It would be throwing money away not to capitalize on those four walls. Besides, Mrs Sperber had daughters, eligible daughters. Maybe two birds she could kill. So word was passed round discreetly that Mrs Sperber would be glad to give a good home to a deserving Jewish young man, and many were the men who thought themselves deserving, who knocked on Mrs Sperber's door, but who, on presenting their credentials, were turned away as not deserving enough. It was not long before Miriam guessed her mother's motive, and to thwart her, she determined, given the chance, to let the room to the next applicant. It was Friday, and Mrs Sperber had gone to the slaughter-house with Gladys, personally to supervise the killing of her Sabbath chickens, leaving strict instructions that any caller should be asked to return in the evening. When the door-bell rang, Miriam rushed to open the door. He was short, a head shorter than Miriam, so that she could see over and beyond him, a fact that pleased her immediately. Eyes—grey, hair—black, profession—none, special peculiarities—none, references—none. "You can have the room," she said. "Come in." He carried a violin-case under one arm and a shabby brown paper parcel in the other. Miriam led the way. She opened the door to her brother's room and let the visitor pass through. And looking at the room she had entered a hundred times, she saw for the first time how dingy and shabby it was, how over-furnished, and she hated that he should have to live in such drabness.

"Where's your luggage?" she asked, a little crossly.

Shyly he pointed to his parcel.

"Oh!" Miriam wondered whether she had done the right thing. A man with no luggage, no profession, no references, could hardly in her mother's eyes be called deserving. But there was something about him that fascinated her. His eyes perhaps, and the long beautiful face affixed to his short body. "We have supper at seven o'clock. I'll come and fetch you."

"Thank you."

When Mrs Sperber returned, Miriam said nothing. She helped prepare the table and discreetly laid for one extra. At seven o'clock, the family were assembled and Mrs Sperber blessed the Sabbath candles. Miriam slid silently upstairs. He was sitting on the edge of the bed, the violin resting on his lap.

"We're ready now," she told him. He followed her downstairs and into the dining-room. The family were already seated and Miriam showed him to the empty place. "I don't know your name," she said, realizing it for the first time. "But this," she turned to her family, "is our new lodger."

Everybody looked at Mrs Sperber. She was pouring the wine and, apart from a slight trembling of her hand, there was no indication that she had heard what her daughter had said.

"Levy," the man offered, but there were no takers.

"Sit down," Miriam told him, and she placed him by her side. This was her charge and against the silent antagonism of her family she would defend him. The meal was long and silent. Even Benny behaved himself, glaring sideways occasionally at the new acquisition. After supper, the parents settled down by the fire and the girls cleared the table. Mr Levy erased himself, and with a hint of a smile at Miriam, he backed out of the

29

room. Miriam stood staring after him and waiting for her mother's onslaught. But not a word was said. Mrs Sperber had, for some reason or another, accepted him.

Saturday was a day of rest in the Sperber household. After breakfast, the family dressed for the synagogue and Mr Levy returned to his room. Miriam waited for him. Surely he must be going to the synagogue too. A few minutes later, he reappeared at the top of the stairway, a wooden tray strung to his neck. As he descended, Miriam could see its contents; matches, hairpins, bootlaces and a few combs. He smiled at her again and, without a word, left the house.

Miriam rushed to the window to look after him. Along the river and to the steps of the bridge. When he reached the middle of the bridge, he stopped. One or two passers-by stopped to buy something, but most passed without noticing him.

"We'll be late," her mother called. "Are you ready, Miriam?"

"Yes, Mama, I'm coming."

When they returned a few hours later, Miriam rushed into the dining-room and drew back the curtain. There he stood still, in exactly the same position as she had left him and along the water and up the forty-five stone steps to the middle of the bridge, she steered a thought towards him, and suddenly he turned and made his way back to the house.

During the months that followed, little became known about Mr Levy, except for snippets Mrs Sperber had gathered during short conversations on the stairs.

His English was poor, and his Yiddish was of the European brand which Mrs Sperber found hard to follow. The children spoke no Yiddish, and Mr Sperber was a silent man. He treated Mr Levy with the silent respect he showed one of his tailor's dummies. So his wife was the only go-between. Over a period of six months, the information filtered through that Mr Levy had come straight from Riga, where there were no prospects for a young man. He had left behind his father and four brothers and sisters. " And your mother? " Mrs Sperber ventured. " Dead," returned Mr Levy. " God rest her soul," echoed Mrs Sperber, who already felt herself one of his family. " And your father. What does he do? " she wheedled. Mr Levy's reply, repeated several times, left her very confused, but after discreet consultations with the more linguistically talented of her friends, she was bound to admit that Mr Levy's father was a horse-thief.

Mr Levy's routine never varied. Every day after breakfast, he would go out with his tray, every day except Sunday which he would spend in his room playing the violin. Miriam brought him down to every meal, and as he withdrew afterwards, he always smiled at her. On her way home from school, she would make a detour over the bridge and as she passed he would smile at her again. None of the family made any comment on his mode of livelihood; there was neither contempt nor curiosity. Just a silent acceptance.

One Saturday morning he crossed Miriam on the stairs as he was going out to work. He stopped a step above her so that they were on a level, and taking a gilded comb from the tray, he offered it to her. She took it silently. When he reached the foot of the stairway, he turned towards her. "Miriam," he said. It was the first time he had called her by her name. "Will you marry me?"

"Yes, Mr Levy."

Where Miriam was concerned, Mrs Sperber knew better than to argue or question. Within a month they were married and there were two paying-guests in Mrs Sperber's house.

One morning, shortly afterwards, the postman delivered calling-up papers for Mr Levy. Mrs Sperber never understood how it got to be known that anyone eligible for conscription could be found anywhere, and she marvelled at the organization that could track down so seemingly an insignificant person as Mr Levy. His presence in the army, she considered, could make absolutely no difference to the outcome of the war. Something had to be done.

On such occasions, when a decision had to be taken, a family conference was called. And although most of the family were present, Mr Sperber dozing in the big armchair, Mrs Sperber only allowed herself to speak.

"There's Mrs Schnitter, of course," she said. Miriam winced.

"But he's a violinist. He'd never be able to play again."

"There's a war on," Mrs Sperber announced authoritatively, as if breaking the news to the world for the first time. "I ought to know. Don't I have a meshuggana son in the army? D'you think I wouldn't have sent him to Mrs Schnitter, and Benny, God forbid, will go to her too, if the war's still on."

"Who," asked Mr Levy, who felt the right to participate in a discussion concerning his own future, "is this Mrs Schnitter?"

The family cowered. Not even Mrs Sperber dared speak aloud of Mrs Schnitter's profession. Mr Sperber grunted, but it was difficult to interpret the nature of the noise. Whether it was one of reassurance or contempt, or perhaps it signified a transition from a light sleep into a deeper one. Mrs Sperber took it upon herself to explain.

"Mrs Schnitter," she faltered, and lapsed into Yiddish, in which tongue she felt safer. But suddenly she realized you couldn't use a holy tongue this way and that anything unpleasant to be said was best said in the stranger's language. "Mrs Schnitter's all right," she said. "She's done lots of boys favours. A roaring trade she's done since the war. She's cheap too."

Mr Levy, whose English was not good enough to discern double meanings, grew red with anger.

"How can you suggest it?" he begged. "And in front of Miriam too."

"Lots of married men have been to her," Mrs Sperber said, "and with their wives' consent too."

"But they're not all violinists," Miriam said. "Hillel's different."

"What difference does it make if I'm a violinist?" screamed Hillel, completely lost in the confusion of the argument.

"Because a finger or so less to someone else won't make all that difference."

"A finger," Hillel whispered. Slowly he understood.

"Trigger-fitter-Schnitter. That's what the boys call her," laughed Benny.

"Never," said Mr Levy.

"It's painless," Mrs Sperber persuaded. "Just the top of the first finger. You lie in bed for a week and then you go about your own business with no one to interfere with you."

"And you can learn to play the mouth-organ," Benny consoled. "I can get you one wholesale."

"No," said Miriam adamantly. "I won't let him do it."

"Then it's Ireland," Mrs Sperber decided. She had done her best. "You know what that means, of course," she threatened. "Miriam will have to stay here and God knows how you'll make a living over there when thousands of boys are trying to do the same. Here, you could go about your business, you could be with Miriam, you could start a family. So you've lost a finger. D'you earn your living with your finger? This, you earn your living with," she shouted, pointing to her head.

"There's no point in arguing, Mama," said Miriam. "We've decided."

It was not often in the family conferences in that neighbourhood, that in the Schnitter v. Ireland battle, Mrs Schnitter came off the loser. For once she had lost a customer to her precarious rival overseas.

Mrs Sperber hovered round her son-in-law while he

34

packed. "Going to all this trouble for nothing," she muttered. Mr Levy handed her his violin to hold while he locked his case. She was half inclined to drop it so that his journey would be less necessary, but the trust he had suddenly placed in her dissuaded her. He really was a fine man, this Mr Levy. Pity her Sol didn't play the violin too.

When Mr Levy was half way across the seas, news came through that the war had ended. Not in the least perturbed at the inconvenience he had been put to, he reached the other side and reserved a passage on the next boat home. On his arrival, Mr Levy packed his violin away in the bottom drawer of his tall-boy, and, as if it had fulfilled its moral purpose, it was never played on again.

5 Brina was the third girl in the family. She arrived on Christmas Day, and as Christmas Day will arrive every year from force of habit, so Brina arrived as the annual event in the Sperber household. Brina grew into a woman only because the process was inevitable. As a matter of fact, the only interesting thing about Brina was the man she married. One can only guess why she married him, but if the reasons conformed to the pattern of Sperber behaviour, it was probably because her mother pushed her into it. You see, Mottel was a lunatic. There was no question about it. Mottel was certifiable, if in those days anyone had been in a position to certify him. But what really kept

him out of an asylum was his dog-collar, which set seal and sanction on anything that took place above it. What happened below, he could not be held responsible for, which in any case didn't matter because Mottel was only four foot eight inches tall and most of this vertical was occupied by his head. "A minister in the family is every bit as good as a doctor," Mrs Sperber said. "It gives a kind of security." Security or prestige, whatever she meant, Brina obliged.

At the wedding reception, Mottel delivered an oration which lasted two and a half hours. It covered a vast amount of subjects including ant-eating, tribal practices among pygmies, the theory of Euclid, the theory of Einstein and the theory of Mottel, but it all added up to absolutely nothing and nothing seemed to have any relevance to the occasion. Brina fell asleep, and being adenoidal, her sleep was a rumbling counterpoint to her husband's descant. Even Mrs Sperber could stand only half an hour of prestige-bathing, before she too succumbed with boredom and embarrassment. When Mottel's meanderings had abated, nobody noticed. The assembly-room looked like the hot-room of a mixed Turkish Bath, everyone caught off guard, asleep, muscles relaxed, bulging, sweating with surfeit of food and boredom. The M.C. rang a bell for a general awakening and announced that, in view of the lateness of the hour, there would be no further speeches, an announcement which was greeted with general and unashamed relief, apart from a few scattered protests from those who had obviously spent some time preparing their speeches. Sulkily, they stuffed their notes back into their pockets. With slight changes of names and location, they could well be used for the next wedding if they were invited and please God if they were asked to speak.

The bridegroom was called to open the dance with his bride. But now it was Mottel's turn. Slumped in his chair and overcome by the fumes of his erudition he had fallen into a deep sleep, a benign and self-approving smile in the creases of his waxen face.

Mrs Sperber tittered and muttered something about the eccentricities of genius, an explanation which the guests dared not refute. She kicked her husband under the white tablecloth, and Mr Sperber, knowing his duty, approached Brina for her hand, and together they clumsily skirted the fringe of the ball-room in a waltz. There was a general shuffling of feet under the tables. Stray feet looking for shoes to match. At last the bunions nestled in their familiar leather sockets and, with a universal groan, the ladies rose to partake in the festivities.

Meanwhile Mrs Sperber had made for Mottel, but with all her kicks and persuasions, he could not be roused. In her desperation, she called over to Sol, the lobbus, who promptly sat on Mottel as if to extinguish him altogether. At half-time Benny took over. Soon Mottel was forgotten. Benny winked at a pretty girl who was standing alone and he too abandoned his post. Sol was playing dice with the drummer, using the skin of the drum as a table so that the music suddenly took on a savage rhythm. Mr Sperber had gone home, and when everybody, including Brina, had finally left, it was Mrs Sperber who remembered to go back for Mottel. With quiet determination, she threw a glass of water over his face, told him that he was now married and that he had better go and do something about it. Which he did. Within a week, Mottel was showing his mettle.

The core of Mottel's madness lay in his obsession with cleanliness and personal hygiene. If you caught sight of his hands, which wasn't difficult, because he always kept them folded neatly on his chest, as if in anticipation of canonized preservation, you would notice that they were a raw shiny red, the upper skin having flaked away over the years of constant washing with strong disinfectants. He would open and close doors with his elbows and, if the doors were not already ajar, he would be obliged to take his handkerchief in order to turn the knob. The handkerchief would then be thrown on the floor to be picked up by Brina, laundered and used again for the same purpose.

The floor was an area Mottel did not admit to his consciousness, so that anything of his that came into contact with it was immediately discarded, so that if you coveted anything that belonged to him, you had only to throw it on the floor to gain possession, a habit quickly acquired by Brina who in the process stacked up innumerable fountain-pens, bibles, and cuff-links, which she sold to Benny at cost price, which he in his turn would dispose of wholesale. The replacement of Mottel's personal effects necessitated frequent shopping expeditions. Mottel would never touch money. He would hand his wallet to the shop-assistant who would help himself to the required amount, or to Brina, if she was with him. If to Brina, she would deduct a little service commission, and this, together with her arrangement with Benny, was one of the few advantages she reaped from her marriage.

But Mottel was not stupid. He knew that his weakness was easily exploited, and was convinced that he himself could not be blamed for this aberration, so that if people took advantage of it, he was in duty bound to punish them.

At first he satisfied himself by using foul language to Brina, which he later took into the pulpit in order to abuse his congregation. He had hoped to destroy Brina on her social level, but this only got him into trouble with the synagogue authorities and seemed to leave Brina untouched. Through his behaviour she had earned the sympathy of the community and so from the point of view of punishment, his manoeuvre had been a failure. So he took his revenge back into his home.

His favourite pastime was a very childish one. He loved to pinch people. He would ask Brina playfully to lift up her arms as if he wanted to tickle her. Then he would take the flesh under the armpit between thumb and forefinger, pinch it firmly, and slowly twist it till it could be twisted no more. He would treat the other armpit simultaneously, though he would twist the flesh in the opposite direction. Thus, he would tune in to the right station, and the disparity in their heights no longer visible, he assumed his power till his satisfaction was complete.

Mottel regarded all surplus flesh as sinful. It reflected

39

self-indulgence, and since Brina had this vice in abundance, Mottel was able to introduce all kinds of variations into his punishments. The intense pleasure he derived from his methods only diminished when he realized that Brina was acquiring a taste for them too. Other ways had to be found.

One of Mottel's duties as minister was to supervise the killing of poultry in the kosher slaughter-house. But he could not stand the sight of blood, human or otherwise. He flatly refused to attend to this duty and his living was threatened.

"If you do it once, you'll get used to it," Brina told him.

"But all that blood," he countered. "If only I could get used to it, drop by drop."

So he stuffed a pad of pins into his pocket and suggested a tickling session to which Brina readily agreed. But when the pins penetrated and the first drops of blood initiated Mottel into the brotherhood of slaughterers, Brina decided that this was a punishment she did not particularly care for and that it was time to go home to her mother.

Mrs Sperber greeted her as if she'd been expecting her for a long time. She took a black veil from one of her hats and draped it over Brina's wedding photograph which stood on the piano. As far as she was concerned the marriage was buried.

Gladys was jubilant. "I told you so," she told Brina. "I always said he was no good. They're all the same, these ministers. I'm better off, I tell you, not being married. And who'd look after Mama, anyway?"

Brina was surprised and slightly irritated by their acquiescence. As the days passed, she longed for that element in her life that sustained her, the pity and sympathy she enjoyed, but only as long as she stayed with Mottel. "You can get used to anything," she told herself, "pins too."

And she did. At least there was no monotony in her marriage. She began to look forward to Mottel's newest variation. When she grew tired of it, she had only to express her pleasure and Mottel was prepared to give it a new form.

Occasionally Mottel would have a moment of sanity, and out of this ungodly union, four children were born.

PART II

1 Mr Sperber had been dead for almost a year and it was time to make arrangements for the laying of the stone. Since his death, Mrs Sperber had visited the cemetery every week, always alone, always hesitant, yet always impelled, as one goes to the confessional. This week, she had asked Julie, Miriam's child, to go with her. Julie had not wanted to go, but her mother had nagged her into it.

They left together in the early afternoon. It was Sunday, the strangers' Sabbath, but this was the only day that the Jewish cemetery was open to visitors. You couldn't just "drop in" on the Jewish dead. They, more than the living, had their allotted hour for rendezvous. The gate-keeper was sunning himself outside his lodge when they arrived. He was digesting one of the more lurid Sunday papers. He greeted Mrs Sperber with an exaggerated respect, no doubt because she was a regular, and in view of her advanced years, a potential client.

Like the butcher and the fishmonger, he had imbibed the smell of his trade and the appearance of his commodity. He referred to those lying within his precincts as his residents, for he was on equal terms with the living and with the dead. His appearance and behaviour oscillated between the two states. He had a vitality of gesture and movement which conflicted grotesquely with the strict immobility of his features. His eyes were glassy and staring. A very slight and regular dilation of his nostrils was the only indication that he breathed at all; his lips were dryly ajar, his cheeks caved in, and though they were wrinkled, the furrows were stiff as if they had been ploughed at his birth. His chin jutted out and to such an extent that it served as a pedestal to the rest of his features, an ensemble hewn in rough dry stone, and fixed in eternity. But his hands and body were rarely still. They were as essential to him in speech as was his tongue. He was forever touching you with his long spindly fingers and, after his touch, you never felt quite the same. The weight and feel of his finger was always with you and would be for ever, because you were already partially his. And this was his power. His was the will whether to receive and keep you, whether to tend your covering, or leave your bed unmade, and, although you could only hate such a man, you knew that you had to keep in with him, for he was the Keeper of the Earthly Gate, and his twisting contorted body its yale key.

"Good morning, Mrs Sperber. Lovely day. Good to be out in the open air," he said, and he tapped his foot knowingly on the ground. "You know the way of course."

Mrs Sperber smiled in acknowledgment. It seemed she was loath to speak to him. To look at him was contact enough.

Julie followed as her grandmother led the way. From the gate, the cemetery looked like a maze. A few visitors stood dispersed at several graves. Some were in such outlying parts of the cemetery that you wondered how the people had got there. Had they cheated? Had they crossed over the graves instead of keeping to the tortuous paths between? In adults there is a great fear of retribution, and Mrs Sperber kept strictly to the prescribed paths. Julie followed at a distance, partly because she felt her presence superfluous and partly because she was looking for a convenient grave to jump. One that would measure her leg-span, a little bigger, maybe, so that the actual physical effort would be a challenge, and preferably one that had been there for many years, a grave of long-lying, as it were, covered securely by a thick slab of stone, so that any avenging spirit would find it difficult to penetrate. Although there were many to choose from, there were few that satisfied her requirements. Most were too narrow to satisfy the first need, and the slabs, numerous as they were, were not thick enough to deafen the weakest voice of protest. Then she saw it. It must have been a double one, for its breadth equalled its length. It was covered with a monstrous thick slab of grey marble. A battalion of angry ghosts, armed to the hilt, would have made little impression on that massive bulk of stone. She walked back a few steps to organize a preliminary run, and in a mixture of fear and excitement, took off. When she landed on the other side, she knew that nothing, absolutely nothing, had happened to her. The jump itself had been much too easy, but apart from that, she had felt nothing. No trembling in the legs, no pain, no paralysis, nothing. She was angry and disappointed too. The dead were dead, absolutely dead, and the myth of the after-life was dying inside her. A large crow had settled on the tree above the grave. She picked up a stone and flung it at him. It grazed his wing, because he cawed a little, but still he sat there mocking her childish illusion.

Mrs Sperber had by now reached her husband's grave. Julie watched her standing there, and although she was still at some distance from her, she knew that she was crying. She ran to her side, and they stood there, both of them, silently weeping, each for their own particular deaths.

She did not know how long her grandmother had been talking but when Julie heard her voice it seemed to be spoken in a tone of continuation either of speech or thought.

"I can't make up my mind," she said.

"About what?"

"About the stone."

"What about the stone?"

"Should I lay a single stone or a double one, that would serve us both?"

So this was why she had asked her to come. Julie hated her for asking her that question. She had virtually put her in the position of executioner. She knew that to order a double stone would be far more practical and economical but to advise it was like signing her death warrant.

"I think it's better to have a single stone," she lied. "They look much nicer."

"But then I can't be sure of my place next to him."

"Can't you reserve it without laying the stone?"

Julie had said the worst. She might as well have taken an axe and killed her there and then. Her grandmother looked at her with a look of triumph. Mrs Sperber always wanted to feel that her family wished her death, but she regarded herself, and so did they, as the survivor. She could envisage her reaction to a world from which any of her family or her friends were absent, but her own death was to her a ridiculous impossibility.

She put her hand gently on Julie's arm. "Let's walk around a little, shall we?"

Julie was slightly surprised. She had thought that, once they had visited her grandfather's grave, they could, in all decency, go home. She had not supposed that they would make other calls. But this apparently was part of her grandmother's weekly ritual, and she would visit each grave of those she had known. The order of her visiting depended on three principles; the proximity of their graves to her husband's, for this meant they had died within a short while of him and thus there was greater sympathy; her intimacy with them during their lives, and the various shapes and sizes of their tombstones.

"Let's go over to Mrs Lewis. You wouldn't remember her. She died a few months before poor Grandpa. Poor soul. She should know there's no stone above her. But he wouldn't do anything for her. Got married again before the grass grew. I remember when Sarah, that was her first, was born."

Julie had heard this story many times. The accounts of her grandmother's adventures as midwife, were told under the slightest provocation, and after the first time, the only interest in listening to them, was to see how they tallied with the original telling, and how she would ornament the details. But strangely enough, each telling was fundamentally the same, so that you were driven to suppose that Mrs Sperber either had a very good memory, or that there was a strong element of truth in everything that she said.

"Poor soul. She came running over to me. I could see that she was ready so I said, now don't you worry, Sophie. I'd always called her Sophie, I'd known her for years. I took her home and put her to bed, the place was spotless and he was there running round like a blue-arse fly, not knowing what to do and I said, now you get me some hot water and I got everything ready. I got the cot ready, I got the towel ready, I got the blankets ready and I made everything nice and then we waited and waited and I said how often is it now Sophie, and she said every two minutes, but I could see it was all the time 'cos her face was twitching and she said, Mrs Sperber, it's coming, and I said, I know, Sophie, don't you worry, Sophie, I can tell, it's nearly over and he kept getting in the way and moaning and groaning too. Then the baby was born and I got everything nice and I called the doctor. Whenever I saw her afterwards, she always said to me, you saved my life, Emma, and the doctor said when he came, Well lady, he said, you've done it again. Poor Sophie."

"That's a big stone over there, Grandma. Who's that?"

"That's old Katz. He used to work for poor Grandpa. But you wouldn't remember him. He made a mint of money later on. Went into the tailoring business on his own. But poor Grandpa taught him everything he knew. They were terribly poor in the beginning. His wife had just had a baby and she came crying to me. They all came to me. 'Mrs Sperber,' she said, 'I haven't got enough milk for him.' She was a good little woman. 'Go on,' I said and I laughed at her—I was feeding your mother at the time, or was it Sol?—anyway, I said, 'Go on, I said, 'I've got enough for two of them.' I brought up that baby, you ask your mother, she'll tell you. I nursed him and made clothes for him. Poor Dave, he was killed in the war and she never got over it, with all her money. They're both of them there. That's a double stone. It's nice, isn't it? Black marble. That's expensive, but it lasts. Better than Mrs Ward's. Look," she said, pointing to a grave alongside. "Only been up a few years. See how it's cracked down the side. Just ordinary stone. They say it doesn't stand up to the weather."

They went over to inspect Mrs Ward's unprofitable investment. It was indeed cracked down the whole of one side, so that the monument had lost its balance and leaned slightly forward, protecting the grave, more like a shelter than a signpost. Most of the tombs seemed to beckon one, to come and admire their design and inscription. This tomb reproved the visitor, minding its own business, the business of shielding its dead.

They walked together in and out of the paths, pausing from time to time, while Mrs Sperber read aloud the inscriptions. Occasionally she would amend a phrase, so that it would fit an inscription for her husband. She would repeat it to herself, savouring its impact. "D'you like that?" she would ask and she would declaim it with all the gestures and nuances of the grand theatrical manner. Mrs Sperber had a talent of investing the most banal and sentimental doggerel with some trace of nobility. But since the type of inscription depended on the choice of a single or a double stone, Julie refrained from voicing an opinion.

"I can't make up my mind," she said once again, as she stopped in front of a tasteless revolting black head-post, inlaid with gold and embossed with porcelain angels. "That's Mrs Fegel," she said. "Even she, with all her money. But you wouldn't remember her!" Whenever Mrs Sperber embarked on the story of one of "the residents", she would always preface her remarks to Julie with, "but you wouldn't remember her." And yet, most of those she visited were well within Julie's living memory. It seemed that her grand-mother did not wish her to partake of her private world, that these were people who had lived many years ago, that she had survived them all, and thus, unconsciously, she created her own immortality.

They made their way towards the gate, pausing now and then to comment on the tombs or those who lay beneath. The Keeper was waiting for them.

"Lovely day," he said again. "See you next Sunday, Mrs Sperber," and he touched her on the arm, finger-ing the fur on her coat. He continued to touch her for a long time, and Mrs Sperber did not recoil. She smiled at him, even, savouring his touch. "Next Sunday," she said, "please God." After a whole year of weeks, she understood his power, and Julie knew that something inside her grandmother had surrendered.

They turned right at the gate, which was not the way home, but the way to the stonemason's shop that adjoined the cemetery. The stonemason greeted Mrs Sperber in much the same way as had the Keeper of the Gate and probably for the same reasons.

"Well, Mrs Sperber," he said, "I hope this time you've made up your mind."

Mrs Sperber's face bore no evidence of a decision and there was neither fear nor trembling in her voice when she said, quite simply, "I'll have a double."

In Julie's remembrance, her grandmother had threatened very often to die, but this was the first practical step she had taken in that direction.

2 If only Mr Sperber had waited another eighteen months he would have made his golden wedding. Despite his absence, Emma was determined to celebrate. "He's in my heart," she told Gladys. "Marriages are made in heaven and there they will continue. We will be celebrating together."

"But he's dead. He's even got a stone. A double one," Gladys added pointedly.

"I should live to hear my children say it," said Mrs Sperber.

"And I wish you a long life." With her veiled apology, Gladys had the last word.

The two women were now alone, and the house which had never seemed large enough to accommodate the Sperber way of life now seemed too large even to house its memories. Memories lurk in corners or in the niches of the wall; in the folds of the threadbare carpet, or in the cobwebbed attic. On this greasy patch of wall, where Sol had rested his pomaded head, only minutes after it had been newly painted, the drawer where Hillel had kept his fiddle, or the chalk-marks on the workshop table from the suit that Mr Sperber had made for Benny's barmitzvah. Memories are fixed to their birthplace and need no passage.

"We'll have a family dinner," Mrs Sperber decided.

There had been family dinners before and it was not easy to forget them. An engagement, a homecoming, a farewell, a barmitzvah, any change in the *status quo* of the Sperber family was deified by a family dinner. Benny may be celebrating his manhood on the following Sabbath, but he's still our baby. Sol's coming out of hospital but he'll sit in his old place and we'll try not to notice his scars. Brina's getting married next week, but nevertheless, blood's thicker than water. In a game of catch or hide and seek, there is always a touchstone of security. Something red, a tree, or the shed at the bottom of the garden. Cree, you call it. For the Sperbers it was the dining-table and when everyone was touching cree, the game was over.

"Let's make a list," said Mrs Sperber. "Fetch me a pen and paper from the drawer."

"What d'you want to make a list for? You know the names of your family."

But Mrs Sperber insisted on writing them down. A dying man will cherish his remaining days and cherish them singly. He will not wait seven days to tick off the gift of a week in his mind. He will acknowledge them singly, one by one. So Benny was first inscribed because he was the youngest, and below him, on the second line, Mrs Sperber wrote Solomon and, in brackets, Sol. Then with deference to the male progeny, she left a large space, and wrote singly each on a separate line, the names of her daughters. Then she took another page. In the middle of the top line, as a title, she wrote Family, by Law. Underneath in her smallest writing, she scribbled, Daughters-in-law—two. Sons-in-law—two.

"Let's go and look at the table," she said, "and arrange where everybody will sit."

It was a good enough reason to move from one room to the other and Gladys welcomed it. Most of their time the two women spent around the kitchen table playing with the crumbs left from the last meal and waiting for the clock to chime permission for the next one.

"Where's my bag?" said Mrs Sperber, reaching behind her back. She always asked where her bag was though she knew it was always behind her on the chair. She would never move an inch without her bag. She took out a bunch of keys and with one of them opened a cupboard in the kitchen dresser. She took out a little tin box and, with another key from her bunch, she opened it and took out the key to the dining-room. All the keys were exactly alike and one would probably have fitted all the rooms, but again Mrs Sperber never reckoned in totals. She would never say she had done the laundry. She had washed sheets, she had washed towels, she had washed shirts, she had washed socks. In the same way, she did not have a house; she had a dining-room, a parlour, a kitchen, a bedroom, and each room had its own key.

The dining-room door creaked as it opened, its hinges surprised by use. The two women crept softly into the room as if expecting to find that someone who anticipated some change was already seated at the table. There is something very empty about a dining-room between meals and although the room was over-furnished it seemed quite bare. Though it was clean, spotlessly clean, it had an uncommon musty smell of decay and lack of use. And here, more than anywhere else, memories held to their touchstone. Gladys could still hear her father exhorting Sol to take his elbows off the table and pouring his lemon tea down his son's shirt cuff when he refused to obey. She remembered how Sol had tried to take it as a joke and her father's sudden concern in his fear that he had gone too far. She heard Miriam talking about the virtues of emancipation to her dumb-struck family at her engagement dinner party. Hillel's quiet melodious voice and Sadie's raucous cockney and the monotonous hum of Mottel's eternal after-meal grace.

Mrs Sperber put her hands on the seat of the chair at the foot of the table. " I'll sit here," she announced, as if, after as long as Gladys could remember, she had changed her position. " And you will sit on my right."

Gladys always sat on that chair too, because it was nearest the door and since Gladys was to carry and fetch from the kitchen, this was her permanent position.

The table occupied the most part of the room and underneath it the carpet had retained its original colours. It was the only piece of furniture whose function was respected. The armchairs that flanked it were never sat upon, for the family continued on the hard dining-chairs, patterning the crumbs with the palms of their hands into tidy shapes, long after the meal was finished. The armchairs were of a shiny brown leather, the backs draped with a coloured crocheted cloth, long since faded and offering a protection that was never required. Except perhaps against the three dolls which slumped lifeless on each chair. One was a black doll with a name no more original than Sambo. The sham chocolate glaze of its face had cracked over the years, leaving on its cheek thin veins of pink, patterned like a leaf. On the second chair lay Rose, who had once been a telephone doll, but who, due to Sol's destructive curiosity, had lost the wires of her crinoline and thus also her function, and now she slouched, demoted, on the velvet cushions of her chair. On the third chair, or rather sofa, in pride of place, bolt upright on the stump of his right leg, sat Ahab, the family teddy-bear. Once when Sol had been unjustly beaten, he had taken the bear to bed and ripped off its left leg in a fever of love and self-pity. He had made a less successful job of the other leg, leaving the stump when his fever had abated. The girls had contented themselves with long and patient nibbling, mainly of the ears and paws. And there they sat, the three of them, Ahab, Sambo and Rose, dumbly accusing spectators, disuniting each family reunion.

The sideboard that stood a few inches from the wall protecting in frame the original paintwork was never used as such. On it was displayed Mrs Sperber's silver. An artificial pear lay sadly in a silver fruit bowl, sidling a real lemon, wrinkled, brown and dry. The bottom shelf of the sideboard was occupied by innumerable wine-cups and serviette rings, the duplicates of wedding and barmitzvah presents that could not be passed on since they were all initialled.

"Now where's my list?" muttered Mrs Sperber, holding it in her hand. "I'm sitting here, and you're there," she repeated. "We might as well lengthen the table now," she decided, "so that all the chairs can be put around it." When the table was in mufti it occupied a modest area of the room. For family dinners an extra leaf was inserted. Mrs Sperber selected another key from her bunch and opened the table drawer and took out the crank. Ceremoniously she handed it over to Gladys and stood leaning on the edge of the table while Gladys fitted the handle into the iron rod. As the table expanded, Mrs Sperber was shunted along the edge like a travelling hiccup, staring at the widening gap between.

"Look at the dust!" she exclaimed. It was a remark she always made whenever the table was tailored for a family dinner. A thick layer of dust coated the cross-bars under the table. "Where does it all come from?"

she asked, as she had asked time and time before. Gladys fetched a rag and scooped up the dust into a cardboard box. It could be used later on to keep the fire in. Nothing in the Sperber household was ever thrown away.

The spare leaf was kept underneath the sideboard. "Can you get it up, Gladys?" said Mrs Sperber. "I've got my corsets on." Gladys never wore corsets in the house. Since she was always cleaning and scrubbing, stays would have hindered her. Her body was free in so far as the accumulated layers of fat did not restrict her movements. She knelt down by the sideboard to drag the leaf out. "Mind your stockings," said Mrs Sperber. It was hard to see why Gladys wore stockings at all. They were always laddered and what was left of pure stocking was centred around the back of the knee where there was no strain. The coarse hair on her legs stuck out singly on each rung of every ladder, and the whole effect was that of some dirty comb. The length of the stocking was taken up by the width of the calf so that the garters which secured them lay just above the knee, sunk snugly into the groove that habit had pressed into the fat flesh.

The leaf was heavy and it took some time to raise it to the level of the table. When it was fitted over the gap, it looked like a patch on Sol's trousers, a reminder of the original grain and pattern of the material. The table was dusted again and the two extra chairs were placed at each end of the leaf.

"Mottel and Sadie will sit on these" said Mrs Sperber, before Gladys could make a counter-suggestion.

These were the two most uncomfortable places at the table, because you had to sit permanently astride to accommodate the spare leg in between.

The rest of the family were dispersed arbitrarily. It was impossible to satisfy everybody, the only criterion being that it was preferable to sit opposite someone you'd quarrelled with than on the same side.

"Well, that's that," said Gladys, moving her father's old chair from the top of the table. "We can use this space for extra dishes."

"And where," thundered Mrs Sperber, "is your poor father going to sit?"

"But he's not——" Gladys started. Was her mother going mad? She watched her drag the heavy carving-chair back to its old position. Gladys went over to help her, clutching the chair by the seat. It was cold and clammy.

"Don't touch it," Mrs Sperber warned her. "Hold it from the back."

Together they shoved the chair back into position. Mrs Sperber took out her handkerchief and went back into the kitchen to have a little cry. She sat at the table, scooping the crumbs with one hand and holding her handkerchief with the other, while her mind envisaged her future loneliness that would stimulate the tears. "I'm going to the shoemaker's," she heard Gladys call from the front door, and Mrs Sperber re-spread the crumbs on the table and settled down to wait. She would have liked to have listened to the wireless but she did not like noise when she was alone in case she might miss something. She thought she heard the letter-box rattle. It was too late for the postman, who had already passed their door, and she crept into the hall to investigate. Two eyes stared at her through the letter-box. Then suddenly the flap fell to and the bell rang as Mrs Schnitter's shadow straightened itself through the glass pane.

"I just saw Gladys go out," she whispered as Mrs Sperber opened the door, "so I thought it would be a good moment to see you."

She wore a large black hat with a veil which was slightly creased and through which you could still see the depression of the letter-box on her forehead. Her long black coat was soup-stained down the front. Two red glass beads from her necklace had caught in the second buttonhole and looked like smudges of blood. The varnish had chipped off unevenly on her nails so that her hands looked like jagged claws. In one of them she gripped an old black hold-all, out of which she pulled a worn ledger.

"I've got someone," she whispered triumphantly. "Let's go into the kitchen."

"What's the matter with him?" asked Mrs Sperber.

"Nothing. Absolutely nothing." Mrs Schnitter had taken the question as a personal affront.

"Only?" Mrs Sperber still wasn't satisfied.

"Only nothing. Why must you only look for faults? Two arms, two legs, and money. What more do you want?"

"If he's got two arms, two legs, *and* money," Mrs Sperber repeated, "*and* he's on your books, there must be something the matter with him."

"D'you want to hear about him, or don't you?"
Mrs Schnitter was getting impatient.

"It can't do any harm." And sitting down in her
chair, Mrs Sperber started to re-gather the crumbs.

Mrs Schnitter laid the ledger on the table. The book
held all the accounts of her former as well as her present trade. When the war was over, Mrs Schnitter had
found herself out of work. She could think of no other
reason why men should sacrifice the tips of their
fingers. For a time, she exploited the political crisis
with her trade slogan, "Be prepared", but potential
clients were optimistic and preferred to prepare themselves in other ways. But Mrs Schnitter had customers,
or she had had customers, and customers meant good-
will. She could think of no allied trade that could
absorb her clientele, but the contacts she had already
made would come in handy for introductions. Introductions—match-making. Mrs Schnitter was in business.

With great ceremony, Mrs Schnitter opened her
ledger. The particulars she was looking for, she knew
to be towards the end of the book. Nevertheless, she
thumbed the pages slowly, from the beginning, one by
one, her half-closed eyes travelling down the columns
of figures, savouring the profits of her former trade.
Finally she came to the title-page of her present business
accounts. The long page was blank except for the word
"Matchmaking", written hurriedly and with a sense
of shame in the top left-hand corner. The book had to
be fully opened before you could read the whole word,
but the blank page was sign enough that for Mrs
Schnitter a new chapter had begun.

Unlike the entries in the beginning of the book, those of the new trade were written in pencil. Matchmaking demanded a more complicated form of book-keeping. Figures had constantly to be amended as the market fluctuated. Expenses with each transaction would also vary and were added to the commission. Even the commission itself was not constant and depended on the relative wealth of the client. In addition to these complexities, Mrs Schnitter had introduced a hire-purchase system into her accounts in order to keep up with the times, and in one or two cases, actions for divorce were proceeding before the last payment had been settled on Mrs Schnitter.

One section of her accounts was devoted to what she called "single clients". Normally, Mrs Schnitter would arrange any number of introductions and charge a commission only on the one that was fruitful. But for her "single clients", she would be more discriminate in her choice, and she would charge for each introduction and waive her rights if there were any results. But the section for "single clients" was comparatively empty. Mrs Schnitter was not psychologically acute, neither was her honesty without question. In the long run it was probably cheaper by her normal method.

Mrs Sperber belonged to this latter category. On behalf of Gladys she had been on Mrs Schnitter's books ever since she had started in business, and to date had three pages of fruitless introductions to her credit. Before coming to the point, Mrs Schnitter ran her finger down the columns to impress on Mrs

Sperber the amount of work she had done on her behalf.

"I'll get Gladys off, if it's my last transaction," she pledged. "It would help, of course, if you weren't so fussy."

Her finger came to rest on a name inscribed in red pencil. He had obviously raised Mrs Schnitter's hopes. The particulars had been crossed out with a black crayon, written off, but as deceased or married off, one could not say.

"You made a great mistake with him, Mrs Sperber," she said bitterly. "I told you he'd make good. Went into the fur trade and made a packet. Gladys could have had him. He wanted her. You know he did. But no, he's not good enough for you. Gladys would have made a better wife for him than the one he's got. Came off Mrs Engel's books. Been on her books for years, so you can tell what a bargain he got. You made a mistake with Mr Mendel too," she said, her finger coming to rest once more. "Gladys would have been a widow by now, and with all his money. Ah well, we can't read the future, can we? I don't see I can blame you for Mr Mendel, anyway." She dwelt a little longer on Mrs Sperber's past mistakes. "Gladys is getting no younger," she warned. "It's not so easy."

"She'll be back soon," said Mrs Sperber, feeling she had been accused long enough. "You'd better get to the point."

Mrs Schnitter turned over the page on top of which a brand new name had been inscribed.

"Mr Bernard Bollom," she announced formally.

"Bollom?" said Mrs Sperber, who was prepared to find fault even with the name. "A foreigner?"

"Well, he wasn't exactly born here, but neither for that matter were you."

Having disposed of the first objection, Mrs Schnitter proceeded to the details. "Age—fifty-five." She paused for further complaint, but on this score nothing was forthcoming. The age, Mrs Sperber found satisfactory, so that she was already juxtaposing the two names. Gladys Bollom. It would do.

"Mr Bollom is a picture-framer by trade." Another pause.

"A picture-framer," Mrs Sperber echoed.

"His income is steady and sufficient to support two people in comparative comfort."

"Comparative to what?" asked Mrs Sperber.

"That's what he said," said Mrs Schnitter, "and that's all I know."

Her tone of voice was so determined that it hinted at her knowing a lot more. "Height—six foot. Build, normal; gait, slightly stooped."

"Stooped?" pounced Mrs Sperber. "A cripple perhaps, he is?"

"He stoops like any tall man stoops," Mrs Schnitter defended her client. "Let me finish." Only one item remained. "Looks," she concluded.

"Only?" insisted Mrs Sperber.

Mrs Schnitter hesitated and without looking up she murmured, "Average."

Mrs Schnitter's vocabulary was not large and a man could be one of three things, handsome, average or homely. All that "average" could mean was that the client was neither eye-shattering nor downright ugly. Mr Bollom could have looked like anything.

"Well?" said Mrs Schnitter, challenging Mrs Sperber to find one omission in her thorough diagnosis. "I think that's everything. Now are you interested?"

"I'll talk to Gladys about it."

"You always talk to Gladys about it. That's why nothing ever comes off. Look, do me a favour, will you? Ask him over when you've got other people here so it won't look arranged. Look, Mrs Sperber," Mrs Schnitter clearly foresaw another fruitless effort, "Gladys is no chicken. It gets more and more difficult."

Mrs Schnitter was right, Mrs Sperber knew. "All right," she said, "I've got a family dinner on Tuesday. It would have been my Golden Wedding."

"God rest his soul," said Mrs Schnitter.

"Tell him to come on Tuesday at eight o'clock."

"But Mrs Sperber, don't you think, maybe, it's a bit intimate for him, a stranger, I mean, to come to a family dinner. After dinner, maybe, or another time."

"Tell him to come to dinner," Mrs Sperber ordered. "If he's going to be one of the family, he might as well get used to it."

The sound of Gladys' key in the door put an end to the conversation. Mrs Schnitter hurriedly stuffed the ledger back into the black bag and started to talk frantically about the rising cost of living. When Gladys came into the room, Mrs Schnitter was protesting that kosher chickens were up a shilling a pound so what was the Chief Rabbi shouting about when the Jews bought goyische meat. But Gladys was not hoodwinked by Mrs Schnitter's indignations. Mrs Schnitter's presence in a house could only mean one thing—business.

"And who will look after my mother, Mrs Schnitter, or do you see to that too?"

"What's the matter with you, Gladys? Mrs Schnitter was just passing by. We were waiting for you to come home to make tea. Now take your coat off, Millie. You'll catch a cold when you go out."

But Mrs Schnitter would not take off her coat. The only concession she made was to unfasten the buttons. The coat fell open revealing a beautiful black dress with a brocade centre panel. Mrs Schnitter obviously wore her coat as a permanent pinafore and only took it off to celebrate the completion of a deal.

"Where did you go?" Mrs Sperber asked.

"I told you. I went to the shoemaker's."

"Oh yes, I forgot. Did you meet anybody?"

"Only Mrs Cohen."

"Which Mrs Cohen?"

"You know Mrs Cohen."

"I know a hundred Mrs Cohens." Mrs Sperber was exasperated.

"Cohen, the delicatess."

"Oh, Rachel. What's her news?"

"Nothing much."

The "much" was the operative word. When Gladys appeared casual it signified that she had news of great import.

"What do you mean by 'much'?" asked Mrs

Schnitter, anxious to relieve Mrs Sperber of part of the prosecution.

"What I said. Nothing much," Gladys repeated.

"Well, why do you say 'much'?" Mrs Sperber pleaded as if it were better to invent some gossip rather than to hint at rumours that did not exist.

"Well, nothing," said Gladys. "You satisfied?"

Mrs Sperber poured tea. If Mrs Cohen, the delicatess, had no news, then indeed, there wasn't any.

"You take sugar, Millie?"

"No thank you, my dear. Haven't touched it since my poor Yankel died. God rest his soul. He had sugar, you know."

Gladys was annoyed. She had baited too long. Now the edge of her news would be blunted.

"Oh, I forgot. Mrs Cohen did say something," she tried again. But by now Mrs Sperber knew her daughter's tactics. "Milk?" she asked Mrs Schnitter, ignoring her. There was a long silence. Gladys wanted an audience, but the two women did not want to risk paying again. One side had to capitulate.

"What did Mrs Cohen say?" It was Mrs Sperber who could contain herself no longer.

"Mrs Feigelstone has got a name!"

The two women looked at each other, bewildered. This was the first reaction Gladys had anticipated. On her way home from the encounter with Mrs Cohen she had rehearsed the telling of her news over and over again. The news was too meaty to be thrown away in one sentence, but it could be announced cryptically, to leave room for questioning and elaboration.

"Mrs Feigelstone has got a name?" Mrs Sperber repeated.

"Oh, my God, she's dead," said Mrs Schnitter.

"God rest her soul?" queried Mrs Sperber, looking at Gladys for confirmation.

Gladys was displeased. She had not wanted them to guess and certainly not so quickly. "Yes," she replied grudgingly, "last night in her sleep."

"God rest her soul!" put in Mrs Sperber, who no longer doubted that Mrs Feigelstone was no more.

"She had sugar, didn't she? Oh, it's terrible," said Mrs Schnitter, the voice of experience. "But she didn't suffer like my Yankel. Why, only last Friday, I saw her in the market."

The trend of the conversation was certainly not going according to plan. The two women were digressing, and, if Gladys did not interfere now, they threatened to carry on for hours, discussing the relative seriousness of Yankel's and Mrs Feigelstone's diabetes.

"She's got a name," Gladys said, in an attempt to centralize herself once more.

"Who's got a name?"

"Mrs Feigelstone."

"But she's gone, God rest her soul!" The two women stared at each other, puzzled, and then at Gladys for an explanation.

Gladys opened her mouth and shut it again.

"Well?" fidgeted Mrs Sperber, itching with curiosity.

"Her daughter had a daughter this morning!"

"Oh, so they're calling her Beatie," screamed Mrs

Schnitter, alarmed at her own acuteness. "Beatie Feigelstone dies and Beatie Feigelstone is born."

"Mrs Feigelstone has got a name," repeated Mrs Sperber, marvelling more at Gladys' method of telling rather than at the news itself.

"Birth and Death, that's what it is," said Mrs Schnitter, who felt the need to give some symbolic twist to the situation.

"And marriage," said Gladys.

Mrs Schnitter sensed a curtain line and took her leave.

3 On Monday night when Gladys went to bed she had willed herself to wake up at six o'clock, and when she did so the following morning it was some time before she understood why she had woken so early. First, as on all awakenings in her life, she had to recapture her name, so deep was her sleep, her whereabouts, her purpose, her cause, and thus depression lost no time in capturing her day. She knew, but only vaguely, that the day held something unpleasant for her and she had already finished dressing before this sense of unpleasantness was translated into the family dinner. There was work to be done, a minor spring-clean, so that no member of the family could accuse her of neglecting her duties. The house was already clean, perfectly clean and no amount of spring-cleaning could have made it look any cleaner. Furniture grows old, and dust and grime are its wrinkles so that after

two hours of scrubbing and cleaning the only change that was noticeable was in Gladys herself, who now appeared even more dishevelled and work-worn than usual. She sat at the kitchen table drinking her tea and wondered how so much work could make so little difference. Suddenly she gathered the kitchen table-cloth in her arms and shook the crumbs out of the open window. At the same time the grandfather clock stopped, shocked by this revolution. Gladys decided she would not wind it up. Moreover, she put a clean cloth on the table, and there it lay, crumbless, with the clock stopped. Nothing to do and no time to do it in.

The postman brought letters of congratulations from the family. Sol's card was naturally understamped, so Gladys hastily read the greetings and tried to memorize the verse before handing it back to the postman. She took the other cards upstairs with her mother's tea, so that the crying would be over by the time she got up.

With the cooking and the general preparation, the day passed with little argument. A hundred times Mrs Sperber would turn away from the stove, ladle in hand, and declare, " I don't know why I go to all this trouble," and Gladys would affirm that she didn't know either. Nevertheless, they prepared for the party ungrudgingly. Mrs Sperber had managed to re-wind the grandfather clock, and the cloth on the kitchen table already bore witness to her breakfast, so that the *status quo* was restored. Mrs Sperber had made several attempts during the day to break the news of the extra guest to Gladys. She had laid for one extra at the end of the table, but Gladys had not yet noticed.

70

At six o'clock, when everything was ready, they decided to have another look at the dining-table. Mrs Sperber was nervous. "You see if everything's all right, Gladys. I'll go and have my bath." She got to the bathroom as quickly as she could and turned the taps on so as to drown the questions she anticipated from below. The noise of the taps was deafening. Perhaps Gladys was calling. She would turn them off for a moment. Silence suddenly filled the bathroom. Not a sound anywhere, just Gladys' feet pacing the dining-room below. Perhaps she hadn't noticed it. But she must have. She'd been there long enough. Mrs Sperber decided that this was the case. Relieved, she turned the taps on again and got into the bath to control the flow of hot and cold. When the temperature was to her satisfaction, she turned off both taps, but the gush of the water and gurgles from the taps still filled the bathroom. "Be quiet!" shouted Mrs Sperber, unable to hear herself.

"I won't be quiet," screamed Gladys, beating furiously on the bathroom door. "The table's laid for eleven. Who is it? Why aren't I told anything? Gladys can do the work. Gladys can scrub and clean, but Gladys doesn't have to know anything. Who is it?" she screamed again.

"What are you getting so excited for?" said Mrs Sperber, playing for time.

"Why aren't I told anything?" pleaded Gladys. She was quieter now. Mrs Sperber squeezed the soap-sodden sponge through her fingers. "I was going to tell you," she said, "only we've been so busy. Nobody ever thought of keeping anything from you. It's a friend of

Mrs Schnitter's. Now there's no harm in meeting him, Gladys. Who knows? He may be very nice." She waited for the abuse that usually greeted the mention of one of Mrs Schnitter's clients.

There was silence for a long time. Mrs Sperber got worried. Maybe Gladys had fainted at the thought of yet another body-viewing. Still no sound. She put one foot out of the bath and almost lost her balance and the voice thundered from outside the door, "Well hurry up out of the bath and let me get ready."

Mrs Sperber had not expected to be let off so lightly. She gladly acquiesced to Gladys' demand, dressed hurriedly so that Gladys could get herself ready. Then she went into the dining-room to check up for herself. The room was suddenly alive. Gladys had filled it with flowers. A large bunch of chrysanthemums stood in a silver vase at the empty place at the head of the table. "My Gladys is a good girl," said Mrs Sperber aloud, her voice full of tenderness. She went to the door, crying a little, to call up her thanks. The bathroom door was open. Gladys never locked it, so that her gruff voice echoed clearly down the stairs.

"Well, didn't you notice anything?" The voice already accused her of ingratitude.

"Thank you, they're lovely," said Mrs Sperber, as loudly as she could through her tears. "It was sweet of you," she said again, hoping that Gladys would hear her. "So kind, so sweet."

Gladys was weeping a little too.

"That's all right," she murmured. "I'm sorry about wanting to put the extra dishes there." Her voice filtered into the steam. "I'm really sorry. Poor Papa!"

"Your poor father," Mrs Sperber echoed, though neither could hear the other. "You're like him, Gladys, with a heart too big for your body."

"I'm sorry about those dishes."

"So sweet of her. That's what he would have done," and she made her way up the stairs.

Gladys got out of the bath. "I'm sorry," she said to herself again, and quietly she locked the bathroom door.

"You're a good girl, Gladys," said Mrs Sperber, walking down the stairs again, and in the bolting of the door and the creak of the stair lay the terrible love the two women bore each other.

When Gladys came downstairs, she was embarrassed, conscious of looking her best. Although her arms were fat and flabby, she invariably wore a sleeveless dress. It gave her a sense of freedom, she would say. But the dress itself was tightly fitting. It was mounted all over with sequins, even under the arm-holes, so that the flesh on the under-arms looked like a column of braille.

"You look beautiful," said Mrs Sperber.

"What's the matter with you, for heaven's sake?"

"Well, can't I say something nice to you, Gladys?"

"It doesn't often happen, does it?" Afraid of familiarity, and in an attempt to prevent it, Gladys was often aggressive. She sat squarely by the table and together the two women partook of the crumb-ceremony. When the grandfather clock struck eight, the first visitors arrived, Miriam, always punctual, with Mr Levy.

"Is that the best dress you've got?" She turned at once to Gladys. "Haven't you got one with sleeves? I keep telling you your arms are too fat to leave bare. And all those sequins. Haven't you got a stole or something to cover them up? Take your coat off, Hillel."

The bell rang again. Through the glass panels, Gladys could see the solid frame of Brina, enclosing in its shadow, either behind or in front, Mottel.

"Hullo, Gladys, are we late?"

"No, Miriam's here. That's all."

Mottel touched the tip of Gladys' finger.

"God bless you, my dear."

"What the hell for?"

"Don't talk like that, my dear," said Mottel in missionary mood. "One day you may be grateful for His blessing."

Meanwhile Brina had joined Miriam in the kitchen.

"Is that the only dress Gladys has got to wear?" she whispered to Miriam.

"What do you think of it? Of course you can't tell her anything.—You see, Brina thinks so too," said Miriam, as Gladys came back into the kitchen with Mottel. "Go and change, Gladys."

"What's the matter with Gladys' dress?" said Mrs Sperber. "She looks very nice."

"Oh, leave me alone!" Gladys shouted. "You haven't been here for five minutes and you're already picking on me. I don't want your compliments, either," she hurled at her mother and went out to answer the door again.

"You can't tell her anything," said Miriam.

74

"She's touchy," said Mrs Sperber, "but leave her alone. Listen," she leaned forward, crunching the crumbs between her fingers, "one of Mrs Schnitter's is coming to-night."

"Then she's got to go and change," said Miriam.

Gladys came back with Benny and Sol and their wives. Sol was still trying to convince Gladys that the understamping of his card had been an oversight. "I would have given you back the money," he jeered. "I don't care whether you did learn the verse by heart. I want my card up there on the mantelpiece with all the others. You wouldn't have done it to anyone else in the family. But you can do it with Sol. Sol doesn't matter. Don't you think I've got feelings too?"

"Don't let's start quarrelling now," said Mrs Sperber. "All that matters is that you remembered to send me one."

"She's right," said Sadie, who couldn't bring herself to refer to her mother-in-law as anything but "she". "Let's forget all about it."

Sadie wriggled her figure in her dress. She too was covered in sequins from the small cap on her blonde-streaked hair to the bows on her toe-less, heel-less shoes. There were a few muttered greetings to Lily, but nobody greeted Sadie at all.

"Gladys, do me a favour and change your dress," said Miriam once more.

"What's wrong with her dress? Gladys looks lovely," said Sadie who felt obliged to defend the sequined brigade. "It's a lovely dress. So much nicer than those long-sleeved things you wear," she added, conscious of the reasons for Miriam's objection. "What do you think, Lily?"

"It's all right." Lily wanted to keep in with the family and this was all the enthusiasm she could muster.

"Well, where's the Schnapps?" said Sol, getting down to business. He crossed over to the mantelpiece where the bottle stood. He picked up each greeting-card, read them, and one by one, cast them aside. "Mine was nicer than all of these," he muttered.

"What's wrong with mine?" asked Brina.

"Too much God in it."

"And mine?" said Miriam.

"No verse. And it's a silly picture. Mine had a silk heart on it. A padded heart," he added. Gloomily he filled his glass. The bottle was passed around and Mottel launched into a speech. He dwelt at length on the subject of absent friends, and gauged the success of his delivery by the flow of Mrs Sperber's tears. When, at intervals, she would dry her eyes, sniff, and try to pull herself together, Mottel would mutter something about dust into dust, a phrase which, in his long experience, had proved an infallible tear-jerker. He paused occasionally, either to give significance to what he was saying or to curse Benny and Sol for starting to drink before the toast was finally given.

"Well, what are we waiting for?" Benny could find no topic of conversation that would in any way interest his family and he hated silences. "I'm hungry."

The door-bell rang again. Everybody waited for Gladys to go. Answering the door was, for some reason

76

or another, Gladys' privilege. She would usually rush for the front door before the bell had found its echo. This time, she made an initial movement towards the door, as if from habit, but suddenly she stiffened, and, turning to Benny who was nearest her, she said, "You go, Benny, I've got to see to the soup," and she darted into the kitchen.

"You stay here, Benny, I'll go," said Miriam.

"Who is it anyway? Aren't we all here?"

"It's one of Mrs Schnitter's. Now see you behave yourself."

The bell rang a second time with a timid staccato, as if apologizing for giving any trouble.

"What d'you mean, behave yourself? Don't you start bossing me."

"You remember what you said to Mr Persoff. That's what I mean."

"Oh, him. You've got to thank me you didn't get him for a brother-in-law. You ought to be grateful."

The bell rang again, a little longer this time, with a pleading insistence.

"Can't you hear the bell?" Gladys screamed from the kitchen. "Why don't you answer the door?"

Miriam patted her hair and went into the hall. The rest of the family crowded after her.

"For heaven's sake," she turned to them, "you can view the body when it comes in."

The glass pane of the front door threw a shadow of a headless man. "He must be very tall," thought Miriam, and hoped that, somewhere behind the wooden panel above the glass, leaned his head. He held a large

77

bunch of flowers in his two hands, thrusting it forward as if it were an admission ticket. Miriam opened the door suddenly and very wide to give his vast figure the benefit of a large frame.

She absorbed him slowly, starting with his feet. His shoes were uncracked patent black, and very pointed. His feet were tightly and uniformly together and parted only at the points, so that he looked as if he were standing on one webbed foot. His legs and torso were like an inverted triangle widening gradually across his chest to the vast breadth and spread of his shoulders. And, dead-centre of this upturned triangular base, there wobbled a tiny shrunken head. The neck, if there was one, was invisible and the collar of his coat encased his chin like an egg-cup. He looked like a plasticene model of a man, made by a child who had overestimated its quantity of clay and had lavished the bulk of its supply on the body alone.

"I'm Mr Bollom," he said, when he felt the viewing was done and all that was left was to refer to the catalogue for the title.

"Come in. I'm Gladys' sister."

Mr Bollom was surprised by this immediate reference to the subject of his visit. "I'm glad to meet you," he said, propelling his points through the door.

"And if you come into the breakfast-room, you'll meet Gladys' mother and the rest of her family."

Gladys had been listening at the door of the kitchen. Miriam was setting the scene. She was building up the title heroine of the drama, talking about everything in relationship to her, preparing for her entry some time

78

after the play had begun. "This is Gladys' mother," she heard Miriam say. Gladys felt the expectation growing inside him, she saw herself as the great mystery in his mind. From seeing her mother and her family, how did he imagine her? Did he know already that she was fat, that her hair was grey and scraggy, and that she didn't care because she'd spent her life caring for others and that she liked scrubbing and housework and someone to notice and say "thank you"?

"How can I go in now, with all these sequins and everybody laughing at my dress? Maybe I'll go in with the soup so there'd be something to shift their attention from me. Or I could call Miriam. Then at least he will have heard my voice. Or I could walk past the breakfast-room door into the dining-room so that he would see me, sideways, pass by. I can't go in with nothing, just as I am, in these sequins, my arms flapping, as if to say, well here I am, I know I'm not much, but I've got a good heart and do you want me?"

She coughed quietly to clear her throat. "Miriam," she whispered to herself, but, even in a whisper, her voice was gruff. She coughed and rehearsed once more. Her voice pleased her even less this time and in her anger she yelled into the kitchen in her week-day tarnished voice, "I'm bringing in the soup."

The family looked in the direction of the voice as if it had been expected, like that of an invisible announcer at a railway station, urging the passengers to take their seats. There was an automatic movement towards the dining-room. Mr Bollom expressed the wish to wash his hands. Hand-washing was Mottel's department, so he took upon himself the business of showing Mr Bollom the bathroom. Together they went upstairs, Mottel wondering whether the visitor's journey was prompted by hygiene or religious conviction. The rest of the family hovered about in the hall, uncertain whether or not to take their places.

"Mine are clean," answered Sol, to Mottel's withering glance down the stairway.

"So are mine," said Benny, putting them in his pockets. "I've only just left the house. He gives me the willies."

"He gives you the willies, does he?" said Brina. "If you had half his brains, maybe you could say something worth listening to. You give *me* the willies, you and your——"

"Wife," finished Sadie.

"I never said that."

"I know you didn't." Sadie laughed. "I just saved you the trouble."

"Oh shut up!" Sol's voice broke through the bickering. "I'm hungry. Are they having a bath up there, those two?"

"The soup's getting cold," Gladys shouted from her corner, still uncertain of entering.

"Where's a towel?" Mottel suddenly appeared at the top of the staircase, rubbing his hands in his handkerchief. "Why isn't there a clean towel in the bathroom?" Mottel was in a panic. The absence of a clean towel had clearly humiliated him. The family pictured a row of sogging wet, dirty towels strewn all over the bathroom floor. It was a room that never had any function at a dinner-party. "Get a clean towel quickly," Mottel screamed. He was beside himself.

"I'll get it." Gladys' voice surprised them from the kitchen. It was her business to fetch a towel anyway, no matter whom it was for. She passed Mottel on the stairway and stuck the steaming ladle she was still carrying into the crook of his elbow. The hot metal struck his cheek as he tried to take it in his other hand. He let out a wail of agony which seemed to absorb his pain, and, like Moses on Sinai, brandishing the ladle in his left hand, let out his wrath and curses on the Sperber family below. Benny giggled. There were murmurs of "madman", Brina made to go up the stairs to stop him, but Mottel was in transport, beyond the initial cause of his outburst and cursing indiscriminately. "You're rotten!" he roared. "Rotten like the earth. Crawl on it, creep on it, for every creeping thing that creepeth over the earth is an abomination to me. Crawl on your filthy lousy bellies over the earth that bore you, creep from your lust like worms from their droppings. For you have sinned and sinned mightily. There goes the goat," he suddenly screamed, turning in the direction that Gladys had gone. "Give me your sins," he cried and he held out his arms as if to catch them. Then, throwing the imaginary package of iniquities after her, he shouted up the stairway, "Bear them on your head to a land not inhabited. Oh God!" he cried, in an agonized wailing, "I'm lonely. I'm lonely, alone, I say. The beast has it better than I. Although," he laughed, "I saw a man and a beast together once."

"That's enough!" yelled Brina, moving cautiously up the stairs.

"What d'you want, you bitch?" Mottel shouted at her. "Aren't I enough for you? You want a ladle too? Here, take it," and he threw it at her. Sol rushed up the stairs and forced him down into the kitchen. After a while he quietened down. Nobody had noticed Gladys' absence and everybody had forgotten about Mr Bollom.

During Mottel's sermon, the soup was getting cold, and Gladys was at the linen drawer, rummaging for a towel that was both visibly clean and whole. But all the towels were thin and worn and with the brownish marks of frequent laundering. The only passable towel bore the name of the town's big hotel down the centre. In desperation Gladys went to her own bottom-drawer where for years she had collected sheets, towels and linens in anticipation of her day. The whiteness of the linen astonished her. She quickly withdrew a small soft hand-towel and made for the bathroom. In her desperation to find a clean towel her fears had diminished and without hesitation she knocked on the bathroom door.

"Here's your towel, Mr Bollom," she said. She would have liked to have spoken softly but she had to raise her voice in an attempt to drown the blasphemous roar from the landing. The bathroom door opened slightly and a long thin hand dangled anonymously in the crack. "Thank you," it said, opening the thumb and forefinger. Gladys placed the towel in the aperture he had made for her, trying to avoid the flesh of his hand. But her fist holding the towel was clenched and too big to avoid contact. When Mr Bollom felt the towel fabric in his palm, he clasped his fingers together and drew the towel, together with Gladys' fist, towards him. Once they were inside the door, Gladys relaxed her fingers, satisfied that, by being invisible, this mode of introduction was probably the best. And as her fingers fell trembling into a loose curve, she tried to stiffen them and spread them gracefully, arching her little finger and lowering her wrist, trying to transfer to her hand the pose she would have liked to strike with her body. Mr Bollom let it rest gently on the towel in his palm. He noted the brown freckles on the wrinkled skin, the stubby, wrong-ringed fingers, and felt the hard rind of her palm. "Thank you," Gladys heard him say as she made to withdraw her hand. But he held on to it and pulled the towel from between the palms. Gladys arched her wrists to fill the cold vacuum and slowly slid her fingers downwards till they curled over the knuckles of his hand.

"Wait for me," he said. "I'm almost ready." Again fear filled her. If only she could let herself be known by instalments. She heard the scuffle on the landing and the sudden hurt silence of the stairs. She twisted her body round to look over the banisters, trying not to disturb the position of her hand, so that, when Mr Bollom opened the bathroom door, her face was averted, withholding the last instalment of the offering.

"Shall we go down? I'm ready now."

"Yes," she said, not looking at him, "I'll lead the way." "Let him see me fully from the back. Then that will be everything except my face. He ought to know from my body and hands what to expect. I daren't turn round," she thought. "My profile isn't like me at all. Mama said I looked beautiful. I didn't look in the long mirror. I was afraid. But I looked at my face. It's a pleasant face when you're very close to it. He must be only two steps behind me now." Suddenly she turned round to look at him and waited for his face to register shock or surprise. But all he did was smile.

"Don't be shy of me," he said. He touched her on the shoulder. A hot shiver ran through her body, dissolving en route into a slow steady trembling. Her limbs straightened out of their infantile curve and she pressed her hands on her waist, tickling her palms on the sequins.

"I'm bringing in the soup," she announced from the doorway, with a finality that suggested that this was their last chance.

Mottel had by now recovered from his frenzied attack. Tamed and docile he allowed himself to be led into the dining-room. The whole family shuffled into the dining-room and when Gladys arrived with the steaming tureen of soup, that she had quickly reheated, only Mottel and Sadie, whose places had been pre-assigned, were seated, shifting uncomfortably on their chairs, trying this position and that to discover how best to accommodate their newly-found third leg.

"Well, sit down, can't you?" said Gladys.

"Where? Nobody's told us where to sit."

"Oh, anywhere," said Gladys, trying to get to the table to put down the tureen. Mrs Sperber sat in her usual chair and the rest of the family dispersed themselves. Mr Bollom found himself at the top of the side of the table, with Mr Sperber's vacant chair on his left, and Sol very much occupying the seat on his right. Everyone settled in their places and anticipated the number of courses by counting the cutlery. Brina was counting the side-plates. She was sure hers was on the left, but Benny had already staked his claim to it by a piece of bread. If he had commandeered her side-plate, then he had taken her serviette too, and after careful calculation of side-plates, serviettes and people, Brina decided that Benny ended up with two plates, two wine-glasses, in fact, two of everything. She could, of course, take over the plate on her right hand, but that would throw out Mottel and he was bound to make a scene. So she took a piece of Benny's bread and nibbled at it, hoping that Benny would take the hint silently.

"That's my bread you're eating." He turned to her.

"And that's my plate you're using," said Brina.

"What difference does it make?" said Gladys. "You've all got one each."

"Here, have mine," said Sol generously. "I never use side-plates. My serviette too. I don't need one."

"Need one you do, and it's about time you started to use one," said Miriam for Mr Bollom's benefit.

"Oh, he's only joking," said Benny, figuring that this kind of explanation would benefit Mr Bollom more.

"I'm not joking," said Sol. "Lily, tell them. Do we have serviettes in our house or don't we?"

Again poor Lily was torn between loyalties.

"We do have them, of course, but you don't use them very much." She felt she had brought off a neat compromise. Everybody except Sol was anxious to impress Mr Bollom. He was obviously a man of breeding in whose philosophy serviettes and side-plates played no mean part.

"Well, if you can get away without using them," he said to Lily, "why not? It saves you a lot of laundry bills."

A single thought flashed through all the Sperber minds. "He's mean." Mrs Sperber decided to overlook it. There was no harm in economy.

"Serve the soup, Mama, before it gets cold." Gladys' voice was mellowed. In spite of the party's questionable beginnings, she felt well-disposed to all her family. She glanced across the table at Mr Bollom, whom she found staring at her. "I'll do his washing for him, anyway," she thought. "We wouldn't need a laundry." Everyone was quiet now, with hunger and anticipation of food.

"Pass that to Mr Bollom," Mrs Sperber said, handing a bowl of soup to Gladys. "Please start," she said as she started on the second bowl. "It's a pity to let it get cold."

"Is there to be no grace at this heathen table?" said Mottel, standing up and adjusting his little cap. After Mottel's former outbreak, it would have been inexpedient to argue with him. One could only hope that he would not decide to sing the prayer because that way it took so much longer. The other men round the table obediently shifted their chairs back and stood up, placing their serviettes on their heads. All except Sol, who used his pocket handkerchief, which he insisted on knotting on each corner, in order that it would look more like a cap. When everybody was ready, Mottel began. He started with an almost inaudible murmuring. Sol and Benny tuned in with a humming monotone as chorus, occasionally opening their lips in loud echo whenever Mottel articulated a familiar word. Mr Bollom's lips were sealed, with a grim determination which seemed to indicate that he knew the words very well, but was not disposed to say them. Suddenly Mottel broke into song. He had a good voice and always sang in tune, but he loved listening to himself and would dwell long and lovingly on a phrase that particularly pleased him. Prayer, he felt, allowed of endless repetition, and he would repeat phrases, adding new and more flamboyant trimmings to each rendering. Mottel had gone into a trance again and it would have been blasphemy to stop him. The steam had ceased to rise from the soup, and in its place a half-hearted layer of fat had gelled the surface. Brina, whose appetite was ebbing at the sight of the tepid soup, nudged her husband in the middle of one of his more flowery tremolos. The voice quivered a little and the vibrations fell out of rhythm so that he sounded as if his sound-post needed adjustment. To everyone's surprise, he took Brina's hint and as suddenly as he had begun he lapsed into the tone of murmured jumble he had struck in the beginning. The final Amen was chanted by all at the table, even Mr Bollom, with great feeling and relief. The soup was quickly served and as quickly consumed.

"What's for dinner?" said Sol, his soup-spoon still in his hand. Sol was threatening to shame the family once more. To Sol, soups and sweets were restaurant refinements. Dinner was chicken, salt beef or fish.

"You're eating it," said Mrs Sperber, deliberately misunderstanding him.

"The best meals start with soup or some kind of hors-d'oeuvre," said Miriam, anxious to assure Mr Bollom that not all the Sperbers had lived in a jungle.

"You know exactly what I mean, Miriam, when I say what's for dinner. When I ask Lily what's for dinner, she gives me a straight answer. She doesn't say, 'Well, there's soup, or hors-d'oeuvre' or whatever that word was, do you, Lily?"

Poor Lily. It was not her evening. "No," she acquiesced quietly, knowing that she would suffer whichever way she answered.

"I understand you completely," Mr Bollom interrupted. "Dinner is fish, fowl, or meat," he announced in tones so decisive that the argument could not be continued. Sol beamed triumphant. Was it possible, the Sperbers thought, that their family was being put over by Sol?

"It's chicken," said Gladys, who felt that, since it was Mr Bollom who indirectly asked, he was entitled to an answer.

"Well, let's get on with it," said Sol, picking up his knife, like a hunter who, at the slightest hint of prey, reaches for his gun.

Gladys started to collect the soup-plates.

"I'll bring them out," said Miriam, rising. "You can get the chicken ready."

Gladys knew that Miriam wanted to get her alone. She'd probably start on the dress again. Well, anyway, she didn't dress to please Miriam and, please God, if things went well, she could tell Miriam a thing or two. The way she beat that boy of hers into practising the piano. All right, so he's a prodigy. Everyone knew that. That concert he gave with that big orchestra in his little velvet trousers and old Miriam, puffed up with pride and that's my son nonsense. "No, he's no trouble at all," she was saying to her neighbour in the stalls. "It's all I can do to drag him away from the piano, he just loves it so much!" Poor kid. Anyway she'd better leave my sequins alone or I'll tell Mr Levy to tell her to stop nagging me.

"Well, what d'you think of him?" asked Miriam, putting the plates into the sink.

"Think of whom?"

"Oh, you know, Gladys. Now look. There's nothing wrong with this one. And it'll be nobody's fault but your own if you don't get him." She waited for Gladys to re-act in some way to her provocation. But Gladys was silent, smiling, untouchable. "Well, what's wrong with him?" she nagged again. "He's not bad-looking, he's not too old, he's got money and he's got breeding. What more do you want?"

Gladys was carving the chicken. She cut the leg and the thigh in one piece and placed it in a prominent position, so that her mother would know whom it was for. As she carved the rest of the bird, placing the portions along the dish, she whispered the dedications. The other leg with pieces of breast was affectionately assigned "to Sol", to whom she felt a certain gratitude. And because of this, Lily was given a choicer piece than she would have had otherwise. The two wings lay folded and useless on either end of the dish, with their invisible labels, "for Sadie, for Mottel". Her mother would serve them with the same injunction she had used over the years to wing-recipients. "Mind you don't fly away," a remark that would be greeted by a polite titter all round, except from Sadie and Mottel who, their legs twisted impotently round the legs of the table, knew that her warning was but wishful thinking.

"Well, what do you think of him?" Miriam tried again. This was a new Gladys. She wouldn't be provoked any more. She wasn't playing the game. Who could the family play with, if the goat had gone elsewhere?

"Let me help you take the chicken in."

"Thank you." A new Miriam, Gladys thought. "You can take the vegetables."

The dishes were arranged around Mrs Sperber. The steam clouded her face and through the mist only the hand and serving-spoon were visible, as they doled out the portions. Each time the spoon plunged into one of the vegetable dishes, voices wafted through the steam. "Only one for me," or "that's enough for me, Mama" or "I'm dieting, just one." But when the spoon travelled to the dish of chicken, there was a silence of hope and expectation. When everyone was served, Sol, who had been picking at his portion, gave permission to all to begin. Sol had been surprised by his portion, which, by hasty comparison with the others, was very big. He eyed Lily's plate and saw that she had done very well too. Sol was feeling very satisfied and for a moment he laid down his knife and fork and examined his portion to see how best it might be tackled. At his own table, he would immediately have laid into it with his hands, simply because he enjoyed it better that way. Here, what with Miriam and this Mr Bollom, it was different. He must try, at least in the beginning, to use his knife and fork. He looked at Mr Bollom's plate and saw that his portion, though slightly bigger, was anatomically identical, and, as unobtrusively as possible, he watched him come to terms with his meat. His fork he was using as a skewer and his knife as a lever. Sol would try the same technique. He stabbed his fork into the flesh, and then, gripping his knife in his fist, he prised the meat off the bone. But in doing so, he relaxed his pressure on the fork, so that, as he slipped his knife in, his whole portion of meat disintegrated and flew in different directions all over the table. Well, anyhow, he had tried.

"I couldn't help it," he said to Miriam, in anticipation of a scolding. He started to collect his bits and pieces. Mr Bollom was sympathetic.

"I don't think you've got enough room. I'm cramping you. Here, I'll sit in this chair."

The whole family, in one movement, laid down their knives and forks. A table-full of dentures dropped open, revealing undigested pieces of vegetables and meat, as they all turned to watch Mr Bollom making his blasphemous move. He took his plate, star-crossed with his knife and fork, and placed it in the vacant space as if to herald his arrival. Aware of the sudden silence he had caused, he moved quickly, pushing his chair to one side and seating himself with dignity in Mr Sperber's carving-chair. Then he took up his knife and fork and posed them in mid-air, looking around the table signalling that the meal could be resumed.

The heads turned to the other end of the table. Mrs Sperber gently moved her plate to one side. She was very pale, her eyes staring, liquid blue. She spoke softly, with immense sadness.

"Mr Bollom," she whispered, "I think you've made a mistake. Mrs Schnitter did not send you here to seek my hand. It's my daughter, my good daughter Gladys, who's for sale. These goods," she said, beating on her heart, "were sold a long, long time ago, and in good time, not very long from now, they will be returned to their owner."

The family had never seen their mother in such a mood before. The sadness of her voice, the unusual control and her rare dignity, prevented them from protesting at her deliberate misunderstanding. All of them, even Sadie and Mottel, felt a great pity for her, and they all, even Sol, who had hitherto considered him a soul-mate, looked at Mr Bollom with undisguised hatred.

"I'm awfully sorry," he stuttered, rising from his seat and making an attempt to demote himself to his original status.

"It's too late," Mrs Sperber screamed at him. The dignity was gone. Her protests were unrational, and, aware of it, she grew angry. "The man, the gentleman," she insisted, "who sat in that chair for forty years—you couldn't lick his boots."

"Mama!" said Miriam, whose pity was on the ebb.

"Don't Mama me. Have you forgotten your poor

father? Is there a man alive who could replace him?"

"No one's thinking of replacing him," said Gladys, whose thoughts were too confused to put her strictly on one side or the other.

"You too," Mrs Sperber turned to her, "my good daughter, look at him, yes, look at him well, Mrs Schnitter's latest." She laughed bitterly. "Go back on her books where you belong, go anywhere, but get out of my house."

Mr Bollom was already on his way. He apologized with each step he took towards the door, swearing that it was never his intention to become Mr Sperber, that it was all a mistake, that everyone was overwrought, that he would leave his card and Gladys could contact him. He placed it on Gladys' serviette and, in fear that she might hand it back, he quickly left the room. They heard the front door slam, and slowly they turned their heads from Mrs Sperber to the vacant chair.

"Well there's an end to him," said Mrs Sperber, "and good riddance too. I never liked him from the start."

"No one's ever good enough for you, Mama." It was Miriam who started the ball rolling.

"What was wrong with him? I couldn't see anything wrong with him. He only did it to give me more room," said Sol loyally.

"And what's so wrong anyway in sitting in Papa's chair?" Benny wanted to come to the point right away. "It's just being sentimental and superstitious."

At this accusation, Mrs Sperber began to cry bitterly in the hope of warding off further blows from her angry family. But Miriam was not deterred by her tears. "Look what you're doing to poor Gladys. Why don't you think of her for a change?"

Until that moment Gladys had been silent. During the course of the evening, she had felt so many sensations entirely new to her and, as she was beginning to learn to accommodate them, the shock of Mr Bollom's departure strangled all her efforts to speak. But when Miriam decided to take her part, she quickly found her voice and, swallowing the big lump in her throat, she turned on her sister.

"You leave Mama alone. And don't worry your heart out about me. All of a sudden, you're worried about Gladys. Let me get married. Who'll look after Mama then? You?" She laughed bitterly. "Or Sol? Or Brina maybe, if Mottel will let her? Well? I don't hear any offers. Anyway, as far as the chair is concerned, Mama is right."

"You can't talk to her," Miriam sighed.

"That's right, save your breath," Gladys advised her. She was trembling with frustration and disappointment and in an effort to calm herself she made an attempt at clearing the table. But an impotent rage brewed inside her and, taking a saucer in her hand, she flung it half-heartedly at the sofa, where it landed harmlessly on Ahab's head. Propped up by the pillows which the saucer had disturbed, the head fell shamefully on to the hairy chest, the cushions slipped down and pushed the body forward so that it fell folded over on to the one leg, and the deformed bundle rolled on to the floor, where it landed prostrate under Mr Sperber's chair.

There was no point in saying anything. Any word,

any gesture, was liable to be misinterpreted. Sadie's leg had gone to sleep, having stiffened itself against the extra leg of the table, but she was afraid to move it and break the terrible silence. For a while they all stared at Gladys, who looked into the air, refusing to acknowledge them. After a while they became embarrassed and looked at one another, and then, unable to bear each other's accusation, they looked penetratingly at the floor.

"Well, anyway, Gladys, it was a jolly good dinner," said Sol, collecting his bits of chicken.

"Let's wash up and forget all about it," said Lily. Her suggestion was a practical one, but no one moved, each knowing that this was no solution to the problem, that indeed it was insoluble.

There was a general feeling of pity towards Gladys. Having made a physical rebellion, even though it had been a tepid one, she had earned their admiration. Gladys had never fought for anything. She accepted her position because it was given her. She had come to expect what was meanest, drabbest, and most uneventful, as her due. The most she would do was complain. Protest perhaps, but very rarely, and as a formality. But to rebel was something that had never occurred to her, probably through the absence of any wish to change her lot. But to-night she had known desire. For the first time in about thirty years, she had known what it was to want something. Mrs Sperber was silent. Behind her handkerchief, her eyes were riveted on Gladys. Perhaps only she realized that the throwing of the saucer was only a prelude to the next battle that

Gladys was arming herself for. But against whom? she thought. To-night against me. But to-morrow? Miriam? She never got on with Miriam. All of us, maybe, and Gladys alone. But I'll be on her side. She's a good daughter, but she's got a good mother too. Then she thought of Mr Bollom and shuddered.

"Come on Sol, pass the plates. We'll do it, Gladys," said Lily. "You sit down." Gladys was already seated. She had felt her knees weaken, and the pain that travelled from her wrist to her elbow, a pain she had always felt as a prelude to tears, was creeping on her now.

"Come on. We'll all help," said Miriam.

They all rose from the table. Even Mottel and Sadie had managed a standing position. Nobody wanted to be left alone with Gladys and they frantically collected the dishes and made for the kitchen in disorganized clatter. Seeing her family disperse, Mrs Sperber was suddenly afraid. She rose and collected the few remaining dishes. Benny was just making for the door.

"Now, you sit there, Mama, you've had a busy day," and taking the dishes out of her hand, he more or less forced her to sit down again. They're keeping me prisoner, she thought, leaving me alone with Gladys.

"I'm tired," she said, "I think I'll go to bed," and she made to rise once more.

"Stay here, and I'll bring you some tea," said Benny.

"Let her go," Gladys ordered, in a voice that had assumed authority. "Let her sleep—if she can."

Mrs Sperber was already at the door. "Good night," she said, as she let Benny pass with the dishes. "Good night, Gladys. I'm sorry about him, but you understand, don't you? There are lots of others anyway. I'm sorry, did you hear me?"

"I heard you, Mama. Now go to bed."

"Good night, Gladys."

"Shut the door, please."

Neither Gladys nor her mother ever shut doors, unless it was with the intention of locking them. It had a dreaded finality about it, like posting letters. Mrs Sperber was disturbed at Gladys' request, and, though she found it difficult to carry out, she was anxious to please. She turned the knob silently and slowly so that the door would not know of its closing, and, sadly and shivering, climbed the stairs to her bed.

Gladys rose from her seat and went over to where Ahab lay on the floor. Gently she picked him up and carried him back to his place on the sofa. She propped the pillows behind his head and cradled the back of his head with her hand. The hot tears fell freely down her cheeks and on to his threadbare fur. Then, burying her head in his hairless chest, she whimpered, "Ahab, Ahab, what have they done to us?"

PART III

1 "You'll need your coat, Gladys. It's going to rain."
"I don't think so. I'll take my umbrella."

"Of course it's going to rain. Look at those clouds!"
Mrs Sperber pointed an ominous finger at a dark
overcast sky.

"Oh, don't take any notice of those," Gladys said,
slamming the door, coatless and defiant.

They walked up the steps towards the bridge, Gladys
a little ahead of her mother and Mrs Sperber panting
and blowing to keep up.

"When you were a little girl," she mused, "I had to
nag you to come along and keep up with me. Times
have changed."

"Come on now," said Gladys, not slackening her
pace. "This bird has got to be plucked before dinner-
time." There was no movement inside the sack Gladys
was carrying, as if the chicken had already died in fear-
ful anticipation of its slaughter. A newspaper, new and
half folded, was blown down the steps, and meeting an
obstruction, clung with the wind round Mrs Sperber's
feet. She stooped to pick it up, but the wind carried it
away again, high over the steps into the river. She had
caught its black menacing headline.

"It's bad news," she said to Gladys.

"What's bad news?"

"War. It says so in the paper!"

"Oh don't take any notice of that," said Gladys.
"Let's hurry."

They reached the slaughter-house a few minutes after it had opened. But already it was crowded. A long queue of women had formed down the centre of a large hall. Some years ago, this hall had been used as a gymnasium for one of the schools in the town. But there was not sufficient money to meet the costs of equipment and maintenance and it had been abandoned. Rope-ladders still dangled from the ceiling and crossbars martyred themselves idly against the walls; the once-shiny parquet floor was seared with wet crêpe shoe prints and an occasional feather fixed in a smudge of congealed blood. In spite of the noise and the people, the place had the silence and sadness of a children's playground after dark, when the swings swing emptily, when the seesaw is not quite level, when the slide glares shiny-bottomed into vacancy and the castle, half-built at closing time, crumbles and falls.

The hall led out on to a small concrete yard. On the dividing line, and at the head of the column of women, stood a short man in uniform. It was an indefinable uniform. He might have been a commissionaire, a bus-conductor or a park-keeper. Whatever it was, he obviously wore it to give him some kind of authority. As the queue of women moved towards him, he would take their labelled bulging sacks, wriggling, writhing and some resigned to stillness, and throw them on a wagon that stood on his left. The women he would direct to his right, where they seated themselves in the order of their coming along rows of wooden chairs beneath the crossbars. When a wagon-load was full, the queue was held up until an empty one replaced it. And thus the line of women moved silently and staccatoed through the vast hall.

When Gladys and Mrs Sperber joined the queue, they fell silent. Silence was the unwritten rule of the line. A word spoken might have delayed their turn, and all that could be heard above the squawking of the fowls was the intermittent groan of impatience along the line each time a full wagon was shunted away. Then, regimentally, the weight of one foot would give way to the other and sacks would simultaneously be transferred to the other hand. When the women had left the queue to join the gallery of spectators, the silence was immediately broken. Women chatting and changing places in order to sit with the new arrivals and share the latest rumour. There was a continual musical chairs in the gallery with promises to remember the order of their coming. A large body of a woman, dead-centre of the row of seats, steadfastly held her ground. She was impervious to the continual movement and babble around her. Her bosom fell squarely on her knees and she had to rest her feet on the rung of the chair in front of her to form a lap. On this artificial table lay two balls of baby wool, which by regular movement of her knees she prevented from rolling off on to the floor. She looked as if she were playing a harmonium. The voice of the minister could be heard praying in the yard. And, in each pause for the ritual Amen, she would mutter, "One plain, one purl, and two together."

"Baby's bootees she's knitting," said Mrs Sperber to Gladys, taking her seat. "And she's forty-five, if she's a day."

"Mrs Fink," the uniformed man called out, flinging a dead limp sack on to the collecting tray. With great difficulty the woman collapsed her table and gathered her wools into a bag. She had to move sideways to get out and even this she did with great difficulty.

"How are you, Phoebe?" said Mrs Sperber, as she struggled to pass in front of her.

"We're very well, thank you," she said, fondling her belly. "We're just having a little trouble getting out." Mrs Sperber was thus obliged to stand to let her pass more easily. "No shame that woman's got," she muttered, re-seating herself. "Bringing children into the world at her age. And into a world like ours, too."

"What's wrong with it?" said Gladys.

"There's going to be a war," said Mrs Sperber. "You mark my words. I know it."

"What's that you said, Mrs Sperber?" An old woman sitting in front of them leaned back in her chair. There was a creaking noise, but whether it came from the chair or her bones was hard to tell. "A war, did you say? There's not enough trouble we've got."

"It's only a rumour," the woman next to her turned round to make her contribution.

"Rumour. That's what you'd like to think." A woman behind Gladys leaned forward with her offering. "Mrs Sperber's right. It's in the papers."

More and more women joined in the discussion and speculated on the possibilities of war. Most of them were on Mrs Sperber's side. As far as they were concerned the war had already started. There was bloodshed, slaughter in the battle-fields, bombs, air-raids, gas.

The few women who insisted that it was only a scare, and that nothing would come of it, were accused of being shortsighted, stupid and even unpatriotic. The argument became heated; women shouted at each other, while Mrs Sperber assumed position as president and tried to restore order. Meanwhile the man in uniform was shouting the name of the chicken owners until a heap of unclaimed birds lay neglected on the floor. But the women were not ready to go home yet. War was more important than chickens, and first they had to decide whether there was going to be a war or not. Mrs Sperber suddenly had the bright idea of putting the matter to the vote. She had just about restored order when her name was called.

"You get it, Gladys," she said. "I'll count the hands." She took off her gloves as if to facilitate the counting. "All those who say, No, there won't be," she invited. She was determined to call the minority first so that their shame would be silently exposed. A few women half lifted their hands. "Higher," said Mrs Sperber. "I can't see to count. One, two, three, four. Mrs Berkovitz, are you up or down?"

Mrs Berkovitz shot up her hand defiantly with a conviction that marked her out as the leader of the opposition. A few more women supported her until Mrs Sperber, mockingly encouraging the rebels, could count no more than eight. To make quite certain, she counted them again, this time by name. "Eight," she announced, "only eight. How many," she asked, "don't know?" She smiled contemptuously at those who were unable to make up their minds. "Why didn't you say you were counting 'don't knows' before," said one of the eight who had voted against. That Mrs Sperber would give anybody a chance to abstain had not occurred to them.

"I don't see it," said the very old woman in front. "You know or you don't know. War or no war. Yes or no. Simple."

"All right," said Mrs Sperber, withdrawing the chance from abstainers, "how many say, yes, there will be?" A host of hands were raised. "They're so many," Mrs Sperber laughed, "I just can't count." And she put on her gloves to put an end to the issue once and for all.

"We won, though, didn't we?" the very old woman cackled.

"Let's win the war first," said Mrs Berkovitz. "Then we can count votes."

"You want these chickens, ladies, or not?" The pile of unclaimed birds grew steadily higher.

"Oh, we're coming. Anybody would think you had to pluck them."

"Come on, Mama," shouted Gladys, the sack on her arm. "Let's get home. It's late."

Mrs Sperber rose from her seat like a minister who has just won a vote of confidence. She wove her way through the jumbled row of chairs and the bent backs of women sorting out their birds.

"See you next Sunday, please God," she called to them.

"If you get your war, you won't get your chickens, too." Mrs Berkovitz was by no means won over.

"I've never been short, thank God, war or no war,"

Mrs Sperber laughed. "I'm coming, Gladys." Gladys was already out of sight, but the bottom of the sack was still visible as it was dragged round the corner. Mrs Sperber quickened her pace. The talk of an ensuing war had suddenly frightened her. She was afraid and wanted to get inside her house as soon as possible. "Wait for me, Gladys," she called, almost in desperation. But Gladys, clutching the object of their journey, saw no need to dawdle now, and it was not until they reached the stone steps over the bridge that Mrs Sperber finally caught up with her. "Don't drag it like that," she said as the sack thudded step after step after Gladys. "It'll bruise the bird."

"It's heavy. You try carrying it."

"If you wait for me, I'll help you."

Gladys stopped and when her mother was alongside her, she heaved up the sack so that her mother could take the other end. As they carried it down the steps, the sack took on a swinging motion, and, like two in-lawed grandmothers swinging a first grandchild, the two women trundled to Mrs Sperber's house.

A smell of warm blood filled the kitchen as they emptied the chicken on to the table. In order to save time, the two women kept their coats on, and the plucking began. Occasionally, Mrs Sperber would pull at the fur of her coat-cuffs, mistaking them for feathers and when she rolled the cuffs back, she found that her watch had stopped.

"Put on the wireless, Gladys, so's we'll get the time."

Without wiping her hands, Gladys turned and switched the knob, leaving a small feather stuck to the dial. The wireless took a little while to warm up. The humming dissolved into a faint voice and all that was audible was the end of a sentence—"that he has no alternative but to declare a state of war".

"What!" screamed Mrs Sperber. "D'you hear, Gladys? War, did he say? What did you say?" she thundered into the receiver as if a repetition were forthcoming.

"Sh, be quiet," said Gladys. "Listen, can't you, and you'll hear what it's all about." But Mrs Sperber was already at the front door.

"I'll go to the Bergs. They'll know. Their wireless is on all day. There's a war. I told you, didn't I? You wait till I see that Mrs Berkovitz."

The door slammed and Gladys could hear the tail-end of the announcement. There was now no doubt. Her mother had been right. She took off her coat and sat at the table, staring at the half-plucked bird. She thought first of Benny, and then of Mr Bollom, and suddenly she was aware of the futility of schemes and plans for the future, even of the pointlessness of preparing the chicken for the evening meal. She remembered the last war and the heartbreak, the wounded, the dead, the mourning and the drawn blinds; all kinds of images of tragedy flooded her mind, yet strangely enough, she felt no sadness. There was instead a growing feeling of excitement in her that slowly dissolved her first feeling of purposelessness. She saw herself in the situation, as someone whose help was needed, in hospitals, in shelters, in homes. She saw herself uniformed, bathed in other people's gratitude. Her happiness became gradually so intense that she forgot its cause and, looking again at the half-plucked bird lying jilted on the table, she remembered that there was a war and a slight feeling of guilt crept over her. She turned the wireless on again and the strains of "Tipperary" filtered into the room. A new feeling now assailed her, which immediately cancelled out her guilt. She remembered now the flags and the banners, the marches and the parades, the King and the Country, images which crystallized into one idea—patriotism—in the name of which anything, even one's own happiness, could be justified. Now everything is all right, she thought to herself, and, grabbing the chicken by its limp neck, she plucked it bare.

As Mrs Sperber came through the front door, the telephone rang. "I'll get it," she called, colliding with Gladys in the hall.

"It's all right, I'll get it now," said Gladys.

"Let me answer it," Mrs Sperber pleaded.

"If it's for you, you'll have it," said Gladys, the receiver already in her hand.

"Who is it?" asked Mrs Sperber, panting at her elbow.

"It's Benny."

"Let me talk to him."

"In a minute." Mrs Sperber paced the kitchen floor. After all, Benny was her son, and he would have to go to the war. She was entitled to speak to him.

"You make me sick," Gladys was shouting into the phone. "You and your pacifism. You've been cursing the Germans for six years. Now's your chance to stop talking and do something about it. It's all right, I'm not preaching. I'm going to volunteer myself."

"Volunteer?" Mrs Sperber stuttered. It was a war-word in the household and signified the onset of lunacy. "Are you mad? Here, give me the phone." Gladys left her to commiserate with Benny and went back to the chicken.

Throughout the day, visitors called and the family gathered together. The house was filled with the babble of voices, aproned women, speculating on how long the war would last. For the next few days the house became a kind of club for the gathering of women between their chores to share amongst themselves their new excitement. But then, gradually, when no immediate change in their day to day life was notice-able and when they had exhausted themselves and each other with repeated opinions on the state of emergency, the panic abated, and they returned dissatisfied to their homes. "It's not like the last war," they complained. "Everything's so quiet, nothing happens." They felt they had been let down badly. "Wait a while," Mrs Sperber comforted them. She was the last to give up hope. "There'll be plenty of excitement. You wait and see."

Weeks passed before Mrs Sperber's prophecy bore fruit. With a few air-raid warnings and the organiza-tion of a civil defence unit in the area, the first disappointments were forgotten and people began re-adjusting their monotonous lives, though to what they did not know, for nothing basically was changed. Except perhaps in the Sperber household itself. When

Gladys joined the Civil Defence, Mrs Sperber did all she could to encourage her. It was perhaps her way of atoning for the Bollom fiasco. After a few weeks' probation period, Gladys returned home in a uniform, and perhaps for the first time in her life she looked what is known as presentable, for in a prescribed uniform there is no outlet for personal taste. She had already had her photograph taken, beside a white baker's van, which she hoped no doubt would pass as an ambulance, and holding in her hand a roll of paper which she equally hoped would get by as some kind of diploma. The picture was placed on the wall of the kitchen reserved to mark the achievements of the Sperber household. Mr Sperber's tailoring certificate, Miriam's teaching diploma, a photograph of Sol in uniform, Mottel's rabbinical certificate and a small illustrated paper inscribed with Hebrew letters which indicated that some well-meaning organization had planted a grove of trees in Israel in Benny's name on the occasion of his Barmitzvah. The glass of its frame had been cracked and one or two nails which held the paper in place had been bent outwards. Benny had often tried to remove the evidence of his wealth and to take it to the appropriate quarters and offer the sale of his estate. He had studied books on irrigation and the value of trees to farmers to find out how much he could ask for them without appearing uncharitable. When, in his later years, he discovered that the trees were a myth, his interest in agriculture waned considerably.

Gladys hung her photograph next to Sol's. That corner of the wall could be the War Department.

"It's a lovely photograph, Gladys," said Mrs Sperber. "I'm proud of you."

Gladys said nothing. She continued to look at the photograph and saw it gradually flanked with medals and ribbons. "I've got to go back to base," she said, in a tone of such self-importance that Mrs Sperber imagined that great discussions were taking place at headquarters and that no decision could be reached before Gladys' return. "You go right back to your base," she said, echoing the jargon with which she was gradually becoming familiar. "I'll get my own lunch. You don't have to worry about me." It would be a lifetime before Mrs Sperber could resist her leanings towards martyrdom.

Gladys could not wait to get back. She had planned to return at a quarter to one, so that her entrance into the dining-room would coincide with Jack's and perhaps they could, without previous arrangement, sit at the same table. Jack had occupied Gladys' mind since she had joined the Civil Defence. Jack was a short man, and square, with the fat, not of good living or laziness, but of suet puddings and high teas. There was an aura of grease about him, so that he looked as if he were sweating continuously. His forehead was low, and his hair thickly creamed, so that it fell in separate strands over his head and had the overall appearance of a curved comb. Jack was the head of Gladys' section. He wore no uniform. He seemed to have graduated above it, like a doctor, who on becoming a specialist, reverts to the title of Mister. His clothes were badly cut, with overpadded shoulders, and when he buttoned up his jacket, he looked corseted. He never wore a tie, but in its place an old white silk scarf with fringes frayed. Nor a collar. But a stud was fitted securely in the buttonhole, like a label on an empty drawer.

He rode a motor-bike, but, whether on or off, he wore his clips on his ankles continuously. When he relaxed, he would take off his lace-up boots, and, with a pint of beer, he would read a comic aloud, in an accent that was impeccably working class. In short, he represented everything that Gladys had ever held in absolute contempt. But she loved him.

A week before, she had gone to the reception room to collect some bandages. He had been there alone, relaxing. "What d'you want, luv?" he had said.

"Some bandages."

"I've had something in my eye for two days. Can you have a look for me? My wife's tried, but she swears there's nothing there."

Gladys had bent over his chair and looked into his eye. In leaning over, she had raised her heels from the floor, which had set up a trembling in her leg and her body shivered with excitement. "What's the matter, luv? You cold?" he said. "I bet you're not cold," he laughed, "a fine strapping woman like you."

"I can't see anything," Gladys had said, standing upright and trying to steady the shiver.

"I'll stand in the light, then you'll find something," he said, lowering his one leg from the mantelpiece and putting on his boot. He placed himself directly under the naked electric bulb, his one foot shoeless and his collar undone. Gladys noticed suddenly that his waistcoat was unbuttoned. She wanted the light to go out. She wanted the darkness, to hide the stranger that he really was, and she would have approached him and found something in his eye even if she had to put it there herself.

The door opened and Mrs Bass came in. Mrs Bass was a new recruit who couldn't be taught anything. She had been a committee woman all her life and resented being an underling in anything. She had joined the Civil Defence to let these goyim know that Jews could also play their part, and she lost no time in volubly explaining her position to the whole unit, who all disliked her for her over-conscientiousness. At this moment, Gladys hated her.

"Is there no work for me to do?" she said. "I seem to sit around in the canteen all day. Surely there must be something."

Whatever the opportunity was that was about to present itself, it was slowly withdrawn, and Gladys decided to cancel it altogether. "Come with me," she said, "and we'll roll these bandages." She picked up a large package from the table. "There's nothing there, I'm sure. But if it still hurts, you'd better go to the doctor."

"Why, what's the matter?" said Mrs Bass, who felt that, as long as she was to hand, a doctor wasn't necessary.

"Something in my eye," said Jack grudgingly. "But it's all right. It'll go on its own."

"But it may not," Mrs Bass insisted. "You can't play

around with eyes. Let me see." Jack was thus obliged to submit himself to Mrs Bass' examination.

Gladys watched her as she clumsily heaved up the upper lid. How ugly she made him look, she thought.

"There's nothing there," said Mrs Bass, after long scrutiny. "It must be your imagination." Jack twinkled his eye back into focus, and put on his boot. Mrs Bass had settled the matter. He must get back to work.

Gladys waited for the clock to chime the third quarter before she went through the swing door into the canteen. Jack was last but one in the queue at the counter and Mrs Bass was behind him. Disappointed, Gladys took her place behind her. When Jack saw her he offered to collect her lunch tray along with his and asked her to sit down and hold a place for him. Mrs Bass was clearly not in favour of queue-jumping, but she voiced no protest. The humiliation she suffered of even standing in a queue, apart from being out-turned, she considered as part of her war effort. Mrs Bass could be provoked to any limit in the name of her country.

"There's a dance to-night in the Drill Hall," said Jack as he placed the trays on the table. "Want to come?"

"With you?"

"Who else?" he said, slopping the tea from the saucer back into the cup.

"What about your wife?"

"She doesn't have to know, does she? I'll pick you up at seven."

"No, don't call for me. Just blow the horn and I'll come out."

Jack laughed and bit passionately into his cottage pie, but finding no resistance, his jaws clashed together and caught his tongue between. Between gulps and swallows, he managed to swear, stuffing his mouth all the time and washing it down with gulps of thick brown tea. When his plate and cup were empty, he gave a long sigh, unbuttoned his waistcoat and stood up, breathing heavily. A slight belch escaped him. He eyed Gladys, hoping that she had not heard, but not caring to take the risk, he placed the back of his hand over his mouth and whispered, "Manners!"

Having exonerated himself, he left the table. "See you to-night then," he called back to her, "at seven."

"Are you on duty to-night?" asked Mrs Bass, who was seated at a side table and had heard Jack's remarks.

"Sort of," Gladys said, not knowing whether or not there was as yet anything to hide.

"Can I join you?" Mrs Bass was already half-way towards Gladys' table and holding her tea well in front of her. She had sat down before Gladys had had time to reply. "Funny kind of people, aren't they?" she started.

"Who?"

"You know," she leaned forward, "these goyim. Only in it for what they can get out of it. Social life, dances and games. It's only a war could bring me together with people like these. My dear, I just don't have anything to say to them. That Jack, for instance, I don't think he's read a book in his life."

"He reads comics." Gladys laughed contemptuously.

She wanted so much to talk about him, even derogatorily.

"And the way he dresses!" Mrs Bass went on. "Those boots, so working-class!"

"And his shirt," Gladys contributed. "Have you noticed his shirt, with that stud in it and no collar?" Gladys was revelling in the analysis even more than Mrs Bass.

"And his accent! I can barely understand him. He speaks like a——"

"Barrow-boy," Gladys donated.

There was silence for a little while. Mrs Bass, who had sounded the theme, had run out of variation. She could find no other aspect of Jack that displeased her. As a final condemnation, she put in, "You don't find his sort amongst our people."

"Well, it takes all sorts," said Gladys, who felt that on that score she could not collaborate.

"My husband thinks I'm crazy," Mrs Bass confided, "mixing with these sort of people." Gladys smiled at the thought of Mr Bass. He was, if anything, far more illiterate and uncultured than anybody on the depot. He had suddenly, years ago, become a very rich man. His reputation as a business man in the town was thoroughly dishonourable. Nobody trusted him. His language was far cruder than Jack's, she thought, and only his Yiddish broken English saved his accent from being stamped as working-class.

"Well, I shouldn't do it if I were you," said Gladys. "Why should you upset him? There are lots of Jewish societies you can join."

"Well, that's just the trouble," said Mrs Bass. "Why should we separate ourselves?"

"Well, make up your mind, Ena," said Gladys, using her Christian name to soften the irritation in her voice. "If you really want to help the war effort, you can do it in any organization. I've got to go, anyway. Got to make up to-night's rota."

"Wait for me," said Mrs Bass, who was not so easily to be brushed aside. "I'll help you."

Gladys was annoyed. However could she concentrate on her evening, on what she was going to wear, on how she should behave? How could she enjoy her anticipation with Mrs Bass continually nattering about her personal contribution to the war?

"Are you going on yourself to-night?" asked Mrs Bass. Gladys was sure she heard a sneer in the question. She began to hate the woman more and more.

"Who knows?" she side-tracked. "There may be a raid and we'll all be on."

"I was only asking."

Somehow, Gladys couldn't help feeling sorry for her. Nobody liked her on the depot, and perhaps she must have realized it. She was trying to be friendly with her, insisting on the common ground that they had, which Gladys would not recognize. If she were to align herself with Mrs Bass, where would Jack fit in? And at the thought of Jack and the promise of the evening, Gladys felt very tender towards Mrs Bass.

"I'd like you to help me," she said, and as she looked into her face, at the vain efforts of innumerable creams to smooth out the wrinkles, she suddenly saw her rigid and cold and a horrible shiver went through her. "You must look after yourself," Gladys said involuntarily.

"What d'you mean?"

"Well"—Gladys tried to cover up her inexplicable warning—"you can never tell these days."

The afternoon passed pleasantly, and in the rare silences between them, Gladys was able to concentrate on the evening. Mrs Bass was in a confiding mood and told Gladys all about the terrible life her husband led her. How, in spite of his wealth, he kept her short of money, how nothing was ever bought until he was quite certain he couldn't get it cheaper elsewhere. How he swore at her in front of the few friends she had, and flirted openly with their Irish maid. After an hour or two of such intimacies, Gladys felt under an obligation to return them in some way. She wanted very much to tell Mrs Bass about Jack. But Mrs Bass had a long tongue. It wouldn't do for the whole depot to know. The horrible feeling she had had when she had looked into Mrs Bass' face after their lunch flitted over her again, and prompted her to talk about Jack because she felt there was little possibility of the news spreading. She wanted suddenly to take Mrs Bass in her arms.

"You've always wanted to go on night shift, haven't you, Ena?" she asked.

"But I'd never get in it. You've really got to be in with the right people to get on that."

"I'll get you in," Gladys promised. "Go home now, and you can start to-night at eight. I'll fix it with Jack."

Mrs Bass' face glowed with gratitude. "Thank you, Gladys. It would mean a lot to me."

"I've got a thousand pounds in the bank. I'll give it you to-morrow," said Gladys. "To-morrow, I'll give you all I have."

"You're joking about the night shift."

"No, I mean every word I say." Gladys feared how much she meant it, and sensed horribly that a promise was never more safely made.

At five o'clock they left the depot, having made all preparations for an emergency and, when they parted at the gate, Mrs Bass repeated her gratitude, and Gladys' concentration on the choice between her blue or black sequined dress was not sufficient to melt the shiver that once again overcame her.

Gladys told her mother that she was going to a staff dance. In spite of her independence, she still had not rid herself completely of the fear of her mother, and she felt that a dance sanctioned by some authority, would, in her mother's eyes, leave no loophole for the temptations she hoped she would be subject to. By a quarter to seven she was ready in her mother's room. She had decided on the blue dress, partly because the skirt was wider and would be more convenient on the pillion, and partly because the black dress had been witness to the Bollom affair. She crossed over to the window, looking slyly at herself in the long mirror. She drew the net curtain aside and fixed her eye on the road over the bridge. She decided to wait for ten vehicles to pass before she would go downstairs and wait for him there. The cars and lorries came by in such rapid succession that Gladys extended her allowance to twenty, and, when she had exhausted this number, she decided to limit the vehicles to motor-bikes only, and of these, since they were rare, she would allow herself five. The first motor-bike came through almost as soon as she had readjusted her allowance. Gladys could distinguish two people on it. There was no doubt that this was not Jack, so she loosened her index finger from her clenched fist and murmured, "One." The second bike was going at such a speed that it was over the bridge before she could identify the rider. The bridge was empty now, except for the rumbling of the engine, and when this had died away Gladys released a second finger and doubtfully murmured, "Two." There was such a long interval before the appearance of the next motor-bike that Gladys wondered whether she should reduce her limit, but before she could take a decision, the unmistakable roar of Jack's contraption heralded his approach over the bridge. "Three," she said aloud, and a little disappointed. "That's him." He had arrived even before she had exhausted her meagre quota. She put on her coat and went downstairs. She might as well now get out of the house before the horn hooted so as to avoid further explanations to her mother. She kissed her good-night quickly and was just shutting the front door behind her when the unmuffled horn prolonged the drone of the dying engine.

"Come on, ducks," he encouraged her, hoisting her on to the pillion. With legs astride, Gladys' skirt tightened unbearably across the knee. She felt the backs of the sequined studs press deeply into her flesh and she wondered whether the taut fabric would last out the ride. "You'd better put your arm round me," he called back to her, as he settled himself in front. "Just for the balance." Gladys obeyed. "When we turn left," he roared above the engine, "swing over with me. The same to the right. O.K.?"

"O.K.," said Gladys dubiously. She had never attached any skill to pillion-riding and began to view the whole adventure with increasing doubts. She no longer worried about her dress, or the myriad oily pipes that wound themselves about her ankles. If she could just keep on the thing she would have to be grateful. A furious headstrong wind struck her as they took off, and in a second her hair, unwilling or unable to do battle, straightened itself limply over her shoulders. The tears that the wind brought to her eyes as their speed increased smudged the mascara, which was now clotted on the carefully applied rouge on her cheeks. She dared not use a hand to wipe away the tears for fear of losing her balance, so she lowered her head and wiped her cheek on the fur of her coat collar. She wondered what on earth she looked like now. With horror she realized that she had forgotten to bring her make-up with her. Her appetite for the evening was ebbing slowly, when, without warning, the bike jumped to a halt outside the Drill Hall, and with the sudden jerk, the last curl on her forehead which had up till now defied winds, not because of its superior strength but by reason of the clip that held it in place, broke its bonds and fell like a sulking question-mark over her nose.

"Enjoy it?" said Jack, turning to face her. "Bit nippy, eh?" If he was horrified by the way she looked he was at pains not to show it. "Better go and fix your hair again," was all he said.

The ladies' room was very small and packed with women. The queue for the one single lavatory had stretched outside the entrance and Gladys, together with a handful of other women, was obliged to display her need publicly in the vestibule outside. The line moved slowly and it was a long while before Gladys got inside the entrance door. The women in front of her were fidgeting with their handbags or adjusting their dresses, finding any excuse to keep their bodies in movement, while their faces took on a look which expressed their ability to wait in the line for years if necessary. Each flush of the chain was greeted with a muffled sigh of relief from the waiting queuers as they lifted their heels from the ground in preparation for a forward move. At last, Gladys found herself at the head of the line. The woman in front of her had been an inordinate time inside and when the already over-worked flush was called upon once again to perform its duty, it gave a mocking gurgle, a sneer that seemed like the warning of a total strike. The poor woman was heard to try again, this time with even less success, and a weary trickle of water echoed pathetically over the waiting room. Fettered by a social conscience, the woman inside dared not surrender and once again she tried, more violently this time. The answer from the water system was a hearty chuckle that grew louder and louder and almost threatened to resolve itself. The queuers waited with bated breath for the sound of ultimate victory, but the water regurgitated and, like an interrupted cadence, petered out into an ironic trickle. The prisoner inside was helpless. She could hardly emerge and face an already hostile queue, having been so publicly anti-social. Most of the women would have forgiven her this trespass, under the pressing circumstances. Others, the few, were quite prepared to burst as long as it were in the name of etiquette. A divided murmur set up along the line, a few voices encouraging her not to abandon hope, and others urgently imploring her to know when she was beaten. The protagonist decided to give herself one more chance, and, bracing herself, she gave a long hearty tug on the rubber ball, held it down fast, and when she thought it wasn't looking, she suddenly let go. This time there was no response at all, and all that could be heard outside was the impotent creak of the chain as it resettled itself in its usual position. The queuers waited confidently for the next move, their eyes fixed on the door, like a victorious army that knows that the showing of a white flag is only a matter of time. The bolt of the door creaked sideways into " vacant ", and the poor woman, humiliated by defeat, crept noiselessly out of the cloakroom.

Thereafter the queue moved quickly and without formality, and, having fixed herself up with the minimum of equipment, Gladys joined Jack at the bar. He was drinking ginger-beer and pressed her to have one too.

" It's hot in here, luv," he said, unbuttoning his collar and spreading his tie across his chest. " Let's go on the balcony."

A rickety rusted wrought-iron bench, with a spiked railing in front and a pile of firewood behind, constituted the balcony. There was no one there so early in the evening, but Jack did not believe in preliminaries and he intended to stake his claim to the bench before anyone else, whose partner perhaps had been more thoroughly prepared. They sat uncomfortably next to each other, breathing in the foggy night air mingled with the fumes from the paper-mills opposite. Jack put one arm round her shoulder and the other on the top of her thigh. Gladys remembered how, many years ago, she had gone alone to the pictures, and in the darkness and with the stranger by her side, she felt very much as she did now. She looked straight ahead of her, focusing for herself a square in the dark, for a screen. The drone of a few planes hummed in the sky. "They're ours, all right," she heard the stranger say, and, suddenly conscious that she was not alone, she shifted slightly away from him. A few stars appeared on the screen, and then others, dull and slowly twinkling. As more stars appeared they all became brighter, until the twinkling was so intense and the brightness so dazzling that it almost blinded her. Involuntarily she uttered a long drawn-out sigh, which accompanied a warm red glow that gradually filled the screen and the sound of a siren like the whistling of a boiled kettle. "We'd better get back to base," she heard the stranger say and she followed him automatically into the street.

The streets were deserted. A few cars, disregarding the lights, were hurrying home. A fire-engine passed them, ringing its bell, an ambulance in its wake, drowning the noise of the fading siren. As they approached the district of the civil defence quarters, more and more people appeared on the streets, fires were blazing intermittently, the offshoots of the one big central fire at the base.

"Good God!" said Jack, stopping the bike abruptly. "Who was on duty to-night? You made out the rota, didn't you?"

He abandoned the bike in a vacant lot and without stopping to help Gladys destraddle herself he rushed across the road in the direction of the fire. Gladys followed him, hobbling on her high heels and tying the train of her dress round her knees. She saw Jack talking to a fireman outside the headquarters. By his gestures he was obviously trying to establish his authority. The fire was already under control, and access to what remained of the charred building was now possible. Gladys took her civil defence badge out of her bag, and, thrusting it into the fireman's face, she brushed past him into the entrance. Jack shouted furiously after her. Suddenly he had become her superior. "Miss Sperber," he shouted, "you are under orders to remain outside." The few bystanders who heard the command, giggled. Gladys took no notice of him, and he stood there, gaping after her, fixed to the ground with his bicycle clips while his coat tails flapped desperately in the wind.

When Gladys got inside, her entrance was blocked by ambulance men. Four or five stretchers, each covered with a folded sheet, lay empty along the corridor.

"There's nothing you can do, lady," an ambulance

man told her. "Not here at any rate. All gone. Eight of them." In his arms he was carrying an unrecognizable bundle of human flesh, but Gladys noticed the hand dangling from the blanket, the white hand with the lacquered nails of Mrs Bass, whose first turn on night duty had been her last.

PART IV

1 "What are you doing to-day, Gladys?" Mrs Sperber asked as she started to clear the breakfast table.

"I've no plans. Same as yesterday, same as to-morrow. Why?"

"I was only asking."

"Every day you're only asking. Why should I have anything special to do to-day?"

"You're so touchy nowadays, Gladys. Sometimes I'm sorry the war is over. At least, in those days, you were running round and doing things. Busy all the time, you were. Too busy to sit around getting offended."

"And you never stopped grumbling because I left you at home."

Mrs Sperber ignored the reminder of her private Calvary.

"I'm thinking of going into town to-day," she said.

"What for?"

"Well, I'll tell you. I'm seriously thinking of taking a trip to America to see Papa's sister."

"What's stopping you? You've got the money. It won't cost you a penny once you get there."

"Oh no, thank you." Mrs Sperber had been waiting for her cue. "I pay my way wherever I go. I don't cost anyone a penny. I'll start being dependent . . ."

"When hair grows on the palm of my hand." Gladys intoned the chorus.

The door bell rang. It was Miriam.

"She's started again," said Gladys as she opened the door. "America."

"When the hair grows business? Take no notice. You ought to be used to it by now."

"It's all very well for you. You don't have to live with it."

"Well maybe you don't have to for much longer."

"Why? What's the matter? Is she ill or something?"

"God forbid. Look, I want to talk to you."

"What's all the mumbling about?" Mrs Sperber shouted from the kitchen.

"Hullo, Mama," said Miriam, kissing her. "What's all this about America?"

"You can laugh. One of these days I'm going to go."

"Well no one's stopping you," Miriam started and the conversation repeated itself once more. After the final chorus, Mrs Sperber announced that she was going out.

"I know you two want to talk about me, so I'll give you some peace."

"Oh, Mama, don't start again."

"I've got broad shoulders. Don't you worry," said Mrs Sperber, drooping her coat around them. "I'll have the last laugh yet. I won't be long," she said, suddenly conversational. "If anyone phones," she said hopefully, "I'll be back in an hour."

"I had a visitor this morning," said Miriam, as soon as Mrs Sperber had gone. "You'll never guess."

"Who? No, don't tell me. Give me a clue."

Gladys wanted the game to last. The content of news, no matter how trivial, must be exploited to the full.

"Well, he's very nice really, when you come to talk to him," said Miriam almost to herself. Gladys knew that the visitor was obviously somebody of whom Miriam had thought very little hitherto but in whom for some reason or another she was now trying to find some redeeming qualities.

"Mr Corne?" ventured Gladys, with a name that could have fulfilled the requirements.

"Him!" said Miriam with contempt. "What would he be doing visiting me?"

"Is he married?" said Gladys, who realized by now that this would be the key question.

"He was, but his wife died."

"Mr Danziger?"

"Try again," said Miriam encouragingly. She was grateful for the delay. "His wife didn't really die. She was—killed."

"Not him," said Gladys. "What's he doing at your house? He's a crook, you've always said so. No breeding. That's what you say about him. No background."

"Listen, he's not too bad. People talk about him and that makes him sound worse."

"But you're the people," Gladys insisted.

"Look, I'm not denying that he's rough and crude, but underneath he's got something. He's kind. I think he's generous too."

Gladys smiled. "How come so suddenly you find such nice things to say about him?"

"Well, I'll tell you this," said Miriam, angry with herself. "You could do a lot worse than Mr Bass, I'll tell you."

Gladys tried to hide her excitement. The prospect of marrying Mr Bass she would deal with later. At the moment she could not resist pricking Miriam's present vulnerability.

"What would you do with Mr Bass as a brother-in-law?" she sneered. "What would all your nice friends say?"

"They'll get to know him like I'm doing. They'll change their minds. Well, what do you say?"

"What d'you want me to say?"

"Look, I've invited him over to tea on Tuesday."

"You mean to say," said Gladys, not fully satisfied, "that you're going to give him hospitality?"

Miriam had had enough. "How long will you go on like that?" she asked patiently. She introduced a tone of pity into her voice as retaliation to Gladys' sarcasm. "After all, Gladys, what with the life you lead, you've nothing to lose."

Gladys was won over. She felt suddenly very tender towards Miriam. Miriam understood her. In spite of her outward hardness she pitied her, and, wanting to savour the pity a little longer, Gladys put her arm round Miriam and said, "Sometimes, I think I can't stand it any more."

Miriam felt herself beginning to cry. "Well, here's something you can do about it," she said with a laugh. She was deeply embarrassed by the intimacy with which Gladys threatened to colour the conversation.

"Come on Tuesday, and for heaven's sake, don't wear those sequins," she added as gently as she could.

"Are you asking Mama?"

"I'll have to, I suppose."

"What did he say this morning? Mr Bass, I mean. Sid, that's his name, isn't it?"

"He just said he had a proposition to make. He said he was interested in you. He'd always had a soft spot for you, he said. I pretended you wouldn't be interested at all, but I'd do my best to persuade you."

Gladys laughed. She hadn't taken much persuasion.

"Well, let's keep our fingers crossed for this one," Miriam said, getting up.

"I've been unwanted long enough, eh?" said Gladys smiling. She felt that if she agreed with Miriam that she was a difficult piece of goods to push, Miriam would no longer pester her.

"I can't wait till Mama gets back. You tell her. I've got to go."

When Miriam had left, Gladys sat at the table, her head in her hands. Her mother would not be back for some time, so she could allot herself a while for thinking. Gladys would never think during the course of doing other things. Thinking was a separate activity, and could only be indulged in on its own and in solitude. She desperately wanted this transaction to be a success. Not that she liked Mr Bass so much. She had always pitied Ena for being saddled with him. His vulgarity did not offend her as it did Miriam. There were other things about him—his plain physical ugliness— that repelled her. And even as she thought of him as a husband, he appeared no handsomer. But she wanted to marry him for the family's sake. She had fattened on their guilt long enough and now was the time to grant them a reprieve. She thought of the past failures, the chance meetings and Mrs Schnitter's introductions. She remembered the drawing-room gatherings, the potential buyers, the polite veiled refusals of, " It's not quite what I wanted", or "I'll be back later". Then with a smile, she remembered those she had refused, and it was only Mr Bollom who evoked any regrets. She thought of the woman Mr Bollom had eventually found, a woman even older than herself. She wondered if they were happy and whether he ever thought of her. " I'll invite him to my wedding," she said happily to herself. "Please God," she murmured, "let this one come off."

"Miriam gone?" said Mrs Sperber as she came through the door. "She might have waited for me to come back."

"She was in a hurry. Had to get the children's dinner. Where have you been? Did you get your ticket?"

"All in good time," said Mrs Sperber. "There's no shortage of boats."

"Miriam had a visitor to-day," said Gladys invitingly.

"What's so odd about that? A special visitor, was it?"

"Nothing special about him. Nothing special at all."

"Well, who was it?"

"Mr Bass."

"What? That crook? What did he want with Miriam? I wouldn't have him over my doorstep," Mrs

Sperber went on unsuspecting. "Him and his language!"

"How would you like him for a son-in-law?" Gladys came to the point right away.

"What?" said Mrs Sperber, stupefied, trying to conceal her excitement and wondering at the same time how to soften her former judgment. "He wants you, Gladys?" she whispered, playing for time.

"He's interested. That's what he told Miriam."

"Of course," said Mrs Sperber, seizing on the only advantage she could find in such a match, "he's not short of money. Perhaps what he needs is a good woman. Yes, that's it," she said, delighted at having found a line of retreat. "That Ena was no good for him. It stands to reason if she'd been a better wife, he wouldn't have gone off gallivanting like he did. Now you, Gladys, you're different. You could make a man of him. Well, a human being at least. What d'you say?"

"You've said it all. So has Miriam. I'm to be on show on Tuesday for tea. Without sequins. That's what Miriam said."

Gladys did not want anyone to suspect that she was going through with this thing voluntarily, although she looked forward to it with some excitement. She put herself in her family's hands and obeyed instructions.

"It's a lovely house he's got," said Mrs Sperber, who already saw herself installed within its walls. "What more could you want? A beautiful house he's got, a maid too, and money."

"And Sid," Gladys reminded her.

"You'll see. He'll change. If you're good to him he'll be good to you. That's what he wants really, affection and understanding. That's what any man wants. God rest her soul but she never gave him either."

"Well, we'll see. Perhaps he'll change his mind when he sees me. Perhaps he won't be so interested after all."

"What? Him?" said Mrs Sperber, losing control. "I'd like to see a lout like that do better. You're much too good for him anyhow."

The prospect of Gladys being refused by the town's worst braggart was more than she could bear. "But he wouldn't have gone to Miriam unless he were serious, would he? If anyone's going to refuse, it'll be you, not him." Mrs Sperber paused for breath. "What will you wear?"

Gladys did not answer. She pictured the inside of her wardrobe and the sequins blinded her.

"You've got to look your best," her mother decided. "What about buying a new dress?" She threw out the suggestion as casually as a request for a cup of tea.

"*Buy* a dress?" Gladys spluttered. "With a wardrobe already full of clothes?"

Mrs Sperber ignored her objection. "You could do with one decent dress. After all it might prove a good investment and you could always wear it afterwards. I'll tell you what," she went on, "I'll buy you a dress. I'll treat you to one. We'll go out to-morrow and choose one." Even if it was going to cost her money, Mrs Sperber was determined to get in on the deal. Miriam may have arranged the match but Mrs Sperber was going to pull it off.

135

2 Early next morning, they crossed the bridge into the town. Gladys would have preferred to go alone, but she felt that, since her mother was paying for the dress, she was entitled at least to accompany her.

"Where shall we go first?"

"First?" enquired Mrs Sperber, who had not intended a tour. "We'll go to Bell's. If they've nothing there, no one's got anything."

Bell's was the biggest wholesale warehouse in the city. Buying anything personal at Bell's usually necessitated two journeys. There were no facilities for trying on, and goods were released on approval for return if the customer was not satisfied. To Gladys, a dress always looked better on a hanger than it did on herself, so whenever she visited Bell's, she invariably took a return ticket.

"I don't like their stuff," said Gladys. "Why don't we go to Robinson's instead?" The luxury of a retail shop, a fitting room and labelled carriers appealed to her far more than the impersonal label, "On appro.", affixed to a brown paper parcel. But Mrs Sperber was determined on Bell's, and Bell's it was.

Gladys had been right. Even her mother admitted that there was nothing that she fancied. Nantyfallan was the name she gave to most of the goods, a name of a small working-class village that over the years had been throttled by credit drapers.

"Let's go to Robinson's anyway," Gladys pleaded, "just to see what they've got."

"All right," said Mrs Sperber, "but only for looking."

"Supposing we see something we like?"

"Then we'll find out the manufacturer's name and
we'll order it through Bell's."

"But that'll take at least a fortnight."

"Don't worry," said Mrs Sperber. "We won't find
anything." She was already regretting having agreed
to Gladys' request to visit Robinson's. It was more than
possible, she knew, that they would find something
suitable. She would have to insist on disapproving of
Gladys' choice.

Almost as soon as they entered the dress department,
a great mountain of a woman swept down on them to
give assistance.

"What did you have in mind?" She shot the first
question that is always aimed at a client who obviously
has nothing in mind, who has no idea what she wants
and is made to feel thoroughly ashamed of it.

"We'd like to look around."

"What size are you, Madam?" the assistant insisted,
in a tone of accusation. She was not going to let them
get off so lightly.

"We're just looking around, that's all," said Mrs
Sperber, on her dignity. "I told you not to come here,
Gladys."

"If you told me your size"—the assistant was getting
belligerent—"I would show you the rack."

"I don't know my size," said Gladys with the utmost
honesty.

The assistant took a few paces back, screwing up

her face to get her subject in focus. Then she circum-scribed her with a rolling eye and took an inordinate time before giving her verdict.

"About twenty, I should say. That would be our outsize department," she said gleefully. "Up the stairs and first to your right."

"They'll have nothing here," Mrs Sperber muttered, as they climbed the steps to the next floor.

"Well, at least I know my size," said Gladys. "That'll save a lot of time."

A tiny shrivelled old lady met them at the top of the stairs. In her four and a half feet of length she had managed to encompass a gigantic dignity, which was immediately apparent in her smile and gesture. She looked like a duchess who had overdone a diet. By the look of astonishment on her face, it seemed that no customer had made the grade to that department for many years. There was something sadistic in placing an outsize department on the top floor of a lift-less shop, and many a potential customer must have lost heart on reaching the first landing and turned back. There was admiration in the little woman's eye, for the courage of these two outsize stalwarts.

"Come in," she invited, as if to her own parlour. "Do sit down and I'll see what I can get you." She went off as if she were going to put the kettle on, and a few minutes later a mountain of multi-coloured clothes, propelled by two dainty feet, waltzed into the salon.

"We're bound to find something in this lot," she said as she dropped them contemptuously in a heap on the floor. "What about this one?" she asked, picking out a hanger at random. Attached to the wooden arms, a black sequined dress uncreased itself as the little old lady pressed it against her body.

"We don't want sequins," said Mrs Sperber, as if she were going to share the dress with Gladys. "We've already got lots of sequined dresses."

"Well, in that case," said the little old lady, not in the least bit put out, "you won't want this one, this one, this one, or this one." She drew the dresses by their hangers out of the sorry heap on the floor. Gladys sighed wistfully as she watched sequined after sequined gown waft slowly past her. The bundle on the floor looked very dull now without its sparkle. Gladys felt she wanted to go home.

The little lady must have sensed Gladys' feelings, for she quickly dispensed with the unwanted sequins by forming another heap on the floor beside her. From the first heap, she drew a brown dress of no apparent shape, wrinkled and shapeless, without even a button for decoration. She slammed it against her body and held one arm over the waistline to give it a shape the designer had never intended.

"What about this little number?" she whispered, like a conspirator, as if she were showing a chorus girl's get-up with the minimum of coverage. "What d'you think?"

"What do we think?" said Mrs Sperber, spokesman again. "We think it's horrible."

"I think so too," said the little old lady with a sigh and she assigned it to the sequined pile with disgust. "There's this, of course," she said, withdrawing another dress. She placed it against her body with little enthusiasm.

Mrs Sperber rose. She felt this was a good moment to leave.

"I don't think you can help us," she said kindly. "We'll have to try elsewhere."

The little lady was crestfallen. For her the selling of a dress was of little importance. All she craved for was a little company. Gladys was sorry for her.

"Let's have a look at those sequins, anyway," she said.

"Now look, Gladys," Mrs Sperber was angry, "we didn't come here to buy any sequins. You've got plenty of those at home. We want a change," she explained to the little lady.

"I never get tired of sequins myself," she said, determined to hold their company a little longer. "Always in fashion, sequins. You never go wrong."

Gladys warmed to her supporter.

"Let's see them anyway," she said. "Sit down, Mama."

Mrs Sperber was reluctant and with a determination not to buy a single sequin, she sat squarely on her chair.

The old lady would have been prepared to display her whole department in return for a little company, and although Mrs Sperber, seated like the difficult customer on the edge of her chair, did not look as if she were going to stay long, she was grateful for the extra minutes they would spend with her. She took the first sequined gown and spread it gently over the sofa, for she no doubt felt that her own wizened body could not do it justice.

"It's beautiful," Gladys murmured.

"It's just like your blue one," Mrs Sperber was obstinate. "Only it's clean."

The old lady draped another dress over a velvet padded chair.

"Very dignified," she murmured as she smoothed out the creases.

One by one, she peopled each chair in the salon with a reclining sparkling dress, and when all the chairs were taken, she stood in line with her two customers and surveyed her guests. Her face creased with smiles.

"I wouldn't recommend any of them," she said, reluctant to part with any of her new-found company. "The lady is right," she nodded at Mrs Sperber, "sequins are a little dated."

Mrs Sperber gave a nod of triumph at Gladys, who now felt uninclined to do battle alone.

"Come on then," she said sulkily.

Mrs Sperber overdid her thanks to the old lady for her understanding and kind attention. Gladys was already at the top of the stairs and with a backward glance at the little old traitor, she motioned her mother to hurry. As they went down the stairs, they heard the little lady nattering to her guests, "Make yourselves comfortable. I'll see what I can do for you."

"What shall I wear on Tuesday?" Gladys asked accusingly when they got outside.

"I'm quite prepared to buy you a dress if you can find something you want. Let's try the Corner Shop."

The Corner Shop was Oliver's. There was nothing that you couldn't buy at Oliver's from a pin to a peer's regalia. Everything was in one department and the assistants spent most of their time rummaging in drawers and cupboards for the required article. It had become known as the Corner Shop ever since, many years ago, the owners of the buildings on either side had made an offer to take over the lease. Mr Oliver had offered to sell out but he had asked an impossible price, and, although every year his neighbour increased his offer, he would have to bid annually for another decade before Mr Oliver's price could be met. Ever since the offer had been made, which was now five years ago, Mr Oliver had stuck red and black Sale notices all over his windows advertising a closing down sale. "Remaining Stocks must be Sold!" "Ridiculous Prices!" But year after year the stocks were replenished and the prices were no different from those in any other shop. Oliver's stood on the corner, firmly holding its ground, while its neighbour wondered if any other shop had taken so long to close down. Yet in spite of the poor quality of its goods, people flocked into Oliver's from early morning, drawn by the lurid notices of price reduction.

Mrs Sperber and Gladys were met at the door by a dapper young salesman who enquired their needs by the sole means of raising one well-shapen eyebrow.

"Dresses," said Gladys without conviction.

"This way." He led them to the main counter and to an assistant who was serving butter. "I'll be with you in a minute," the assistant promised them. Very carefully, he scraped a slither of butter off the weighed pound. He winked at Mrs Sperber. "Never give overweight," he said, "and you'll be a millionaire." Mrs Sperber made a quick mental note never to buy butter at Oliver's. "Now what can I do for you?" he said, wiping his hands on the sides of his jacket. "A dress? What were you thinking of? Of course you're not quite sure. You want to look around. But that's the last thing you can do at Oliver's." He laughed. "Nothing on show; all in the drawers and cupboards. I'll show you what you want," he said. "Just your size. A natty little number. Coronation Blue." He was unaware of how its name had dated it. Nevertheless, he rattled on, taking hardly a breath between his sentences. "Now, let's see. I can put my hand on it right away." With supreme confidence, he opened one of the many wardrobes, but quickly closed it again on finding it full of gentlemen's mackintoshes. "How silly of me!" he said, as he opened a drawer and rummaged through its contents. "There," he said triumphantly, producing a cellophane-wrapped package. "Just your size. You'll look a smasher in it. You can have it for a fiver. Special price for you, lady." He winked again. "I can sell that dress ten times a day for twice as much." He held out his hand for the money.

"But," Gladys spluttered, "how do I know it'll fit?"

"Course it'll fit you, lady. Fit anybody. Just your size. Fit you to a T." The assistant was getting impatient. He was obviously much more at home with his butter. "You want it, lady?"

"Take it," said Mrs Sperber. Her feet were sore and

for five pounds she felt she had got off pretty lightly. By this time, Gladys had lost interest too, so she automatically took the package out of the assistant's hands, rolled it up and put it in her shopping-bag.

"Well, I hope it fits," she said to her mother as they left the shop. "You told me to take it, remember."

"Well, if it doesn't we'll give it to Miriam. In any case it was a bargain." For Mrs Sperber, this label was justification enough to buy anything.

When they reached home, Mrs Sperber snatched the package out of Gladys' bag, opened it and prepared for the worst. To their surprise, the dress was quite whole and moreover presentable.

"Let's try it on," said Mrs Sperber. "It can always be altered." The possibility of its being an exact fit did not occur to her. Gladys took off her coat and there and then in the kitchen she began to undress.

"Why don't you go upstairs, Gladys, and try it on properly?"

"I just want to get an idea of it," she said. To this end, she did not bother to take off her skirt, so that it was with some difficulty that she screwed her body into the dress. The zip closed quite easily and the buttons. The skirt concertinaed round its tweed lining, but even against such odds, it held together.

"It'll do," said Gladys, tearing it off. "I'll iron it and it'll do."

"Don't you even want to look at yourself?"

"That's not going to make any difference to the dress, is it?"

Gladys folded it inside out and examined the

material. It was such that it threatened to disintegrate if handled ungently. So Gladys screwed it up in her fingers, pulling it this way and that until the weave became taut and split in the middle.

"You satisfied now?" said Mrs Sperber.

"It'll do."

"Thank you for buying me a dress," her mother sneered.

"Thank you."

3 The tea was scheduled for four o'clock and at two o'clock Miriam still had no guest list. She could not bring herself to invite any of her friends, since they shared the same opinion of Mr Bass as she did. In one way, she hoped the match would not come off. It would save her a lot of explanation to her friends. In desperation she realized that the only invitable people were her relatives who knew him for what he was and under the circumstances would accept him. Hillel had washed his hands of the whole affair. He had his own opinions of Mr Bass and saw no reason to modify them now. He was fond of Gladys and wished her to be happy but he wanted no part in marrying her off to a monster. So Miriam phoned her entire family and though most of them took exception to the short notice, knowing that they were last resorts, they all agreed to come and by four o'clock the family was assembled. Gladys was made to model her dress in front of them and all approved except Sadie, who regretted the absence of

sequins. When the parade was over, they settled down to wait.

At half-past four, Sol became impatient. "If he doesn't come soon, I'm going."

"What about the tea?" said Benny.

"We've got plenty for tea at home, haven't we, Lily?"

"Give him a little longer," said Lily. "You never know. He's probably been held up somewhere."

Nobody particularly wanted to mention Sid's name and they were at pains to avoid the subject altogether. So they fell back on bickering amongst themselves. But unlike the usual family quarrels there was no heart in the bickering. Hunger and impatience had driven it out and, at half-past five, Miriam suggested having tea. The family needed no encouragement. They crowded round the table ravenously. As Miriam sat down, she wondered what had been the point of it all. Hillel might just as well come down. She went to the foot of the stairs to call him but her shout was interrupted by the door bell. She heard the silence from the drawing-room as she opened the front door.

"All set?" said Sid as he pushed past her. Without a word of apology he threw his hat and scarf over the banister and made for the drawing-room door. Miriam realized how difficult it was going to be to like him. "I'm here," she heard him announcing himself, "and starving." He grabbed a dainty cucumber sandwich and, as he put it whole into his mouth, he took another with the other hand. His left hand he made his supplier and the right, his feeder. He kept them both

146

continually occupied until the plate of sandwiches was empty. Then he took the nearest chair and sat down heavily. "Nice weather," he grunted. "Give us some tea, will you?"

Miriam inwardly thanked God she had not invited any of her friends. She gave Gladys the tea to hand to him, not by way of introduction, but because she could not bring herself to make contact with him.

"Oh, Gladys, it's you," he said, taking the tea and a large gulp before even setting it on the table. "Well, what about it?"

"What about what?" said Mrs Sperber, who was the first of the family to find her voice.

"Oh, come off it now. We all know what we're here for. B.O.T. Bottoms on the table. Yes or No."

"What is your proposition?" Of all people it was Sadie who took the matter in hand. She was looking particularly tarty in a small black hat with a veil that had stuck to her lipstick and followed the pattern of her mouth when she talked.

"Are you asking me, lady?"

"What is your proposition?" Sadie obviously liked the word and felt it could stand repetition.

"Well, to you, lady," said Sid, "I could make all kinds of propositions. Not here, though. Time and Place," he laughed. Why Sid should suddenly be deterred by such niceties, was hard to tell.

Sadie resigned and her place was taken by Mottel. "We have from the Old Testament," he began, "a very interesting word."

"Oh, I could tell you a few interesting words, very

interesting," Sid heckled, "not in the Old Testament neither."

Mottel was undaunted. "That word," he said, pausing to give added meaning, "was . . ."

" Jesus ? " Sid was anxious to help.

Mottel ignored him. "That word," he repeated, "was helpmate."

"Oh, very interesting," said Sol, who for once chose to be on Mottel's side. Brina beamed at her family, overcome by her husband's brilliance.

"Helpmate, Reverend, you were saying?" Sid feigned an interest in the impending sermon.

"The word is helpmate," Mottel went on, though by now his point was quite clear. "Now it is extremely interesting to notice that this word is a mistake."

"Extremely interesting," Sid echoed, who began to think that anybody who found the slightest interest in such a subject was mad.

"It is the translation that is at fault," Mottel went on.

"Oh, naughty translation," Sid was sympathetic.

Benny had begun to giggle. Mrs Sperber kicked him with her foot. Much as she disliked Mottel, this was no time to make fun of him. But Mottel was too interested in pursuing his line of thought to take notice of any diversions. "The translation gives us, 'and God sought a helpmate for him.' Brethren," he said solemnly—he had obviously moved into the pulpit—"this is a mistake. And do you know why it is a mistake ? "

"I don't know why, and I don't bloody well care."

Sid had had enough. "I had ten bob on the three-thirty this afternoon, and I want to go out and get a paper."

"My son," Mottel said, touching Sid on the shoulder.

"Your son, my foot," Sid was indignant. "I may be a bastard, but thank God it wasn't your fault."

"Oh stop it, both of you," Miriam shouted. "Let's sit down, all of us, civilly, and have tea. This is not a market-place, neither is it a place of worship." She felt she had embraced both sides in her reprimand.

The door opened silently and Hillel came in. He could never take the smile out of his eyes, but his face was very sad. He was obviously making an attempt to control himself and to hide his contempt from the visitor. His hands behind his back, he walked over to where Sid sat. "Mr Bass," he began, very softly and gently, "you are not welcome in my house. I would be glad if you left."

"Listen, cock," said Sid, standing up. "I didn't come here to see you. Nor your wife, nor any of your lousy family. Except Gladys. I came here to see Gladys, and why we didn't arrange to meet on the bridge, I don't know. Gladys," he said, authoritatively, "come outside."

Gladys followed him dumbly into the hall, and on the whole the family were relieved that the final responsibility had been taken out of their hands.

"Sh," said Sol as the chatter started again. "Let's listen to what they're saying." Hillel moved towards the door and shut it firmly.

"Miriam, dear," he said. "I'd like some tea." She

went over to him and kissed him on the forehead. Benny turned to Sadie.

"Well, dear, you see, you could have done a lot worse."

"You too," echoed Sol to Lily.

"I couldn't have done any better. God rest his soul." Mrs Sperber burst into tears.

There was silence in the room now, only because of the sadness no one used it to eavesdrop on the couple in the hall. Suddenly the front door slammed and Gladys returned.

"I'll take him," she said, as automatically as she had taken the dress a few days ago.

"On your own head," said Hillel.

"God bless you," said Mottel. If ever a blessing were called for, it was now, and Mottel could not resist his own particular sanction.

"God help you," was Benny's contribution.

"Amen," said Sol.

Everyone was eager to know from Gladys what the next move was to be. But knowing Hillel's attitude and in his presence, they had more respect for him than to pursue the subject. Silently they continued eating, though with little appetite, for, in Hillel's company, they all felt a little ashamed. They waited for him to retire. But he wanted no prolongation of the subject in his house. He was determined to remain until the last guest had gone. When his intentions became clear, the family prepared to go, contriving to leave together in order to gather again outside the front door. Miriam saw them out and closed the door behind her, and they all stood whispering on the porch. "He's even worse than I expected," Sol whispered to Benny. Gladys overheard.

"He knows you don't like him. That's why he's rude. He's all right when you get him alone. He'll do."

"You definitely said yes?" asked Mrs Sperber.

"Yes."

The family made mental preparations to accept Sid as a brother-in-law. He had to be kept within the bounds of the family. To introduce him to one's circle of friends was indecent exposure.

"When are you seeing him?" Sol asked.

"To-night, on the bridge, where we should have met in the first place."

"You don't think I enjoyed that tea-party?" Miriam was hurt at the ingratitude. "I'll think twice before I come to the wedding."

It was the cue for another family bicker, which developed passionately until the subject of Sid was forgotten and they all went their separate ways, cursing each other.

On their way home, Mrs Sperber nagged Gladys with questions. Even she was beginning to doubt whether such a marriage were desirable. But Gladys was incommunicative. The most she would say was, "He'll do."

He had arranged to pick her up on the bridge at ten o'clock. She was a little late, deliberately, and as he saw her at the top of the steps, he blew his horn impatiently. She opened the car door herself. It swayed to the side as she stepped in and then rocked gently back on its axle as she settled herself in the seat beside him. Sid turned off the engine and put the ignition key in his pocket. He was obviously going to stay on the spot.

"I've been thinking," he said. "Next week I can't manage. I've got to go to London to see my daughter. She won't like it very much, but I'll fix her. The week after that. On the Sunday. O.K.?"

"That'll do," said Gladys.

"Tell your mother, and she can fix everything." He took the key out of his pocket and started the engine. In the silence he drove her the few yards to her home. When he stopped at her door, he took a small brown paper package out of his trouser pocket. "You'd better have this," he said. "You might as well have it now."

Gladys opened the package and found inside a large diamond ring. She shuddered as she looked at it and remembered where she had seen it last. It belonged to a white hand with lacquered nails that had dangled over a blanket a few years ago.

4 The family tried to keep the engagement to themselves, but they knew that sooner or later the news would spread. The day before the wedding, the local paper announced in its headline that The King of Crusts was to re-wed. The article carried some crude references to Mr Bass, knowing which side his bread was buttered, allusions to half a loaf and the staff of life nonsense; in short, reportage hardly complimentary

either to Mr Bass or to his bride. The town did not like Mr Bass, not only because he had made good, but because he had done so at other people's expense.

He had come over from Russia before the first World War, and, like other immigrants of his time, he started as a pedlar. One cold winter's day, his tray full of unsold notions, tired and hungry, he passed a baker's shop. The smell of new-baked bread was stronger than his pride, which, in those early days of privation, he had in large measure, so he went in and begged a crust of bread. "Help yourself," shouted the baker, pointing to a bin of burnt loaves. The crust of the bread was black so Mr Bass took a penknife from his tray and scraped the bread until it was a hard respectable brown. As he was scraping, he realized that in these burnt loaves there was the beginning of a business. Quickly he put the scraped bread at the bottom of the bin out of sight, picked up a badly burned loaf and began to eat it.

"What d'you do with this bread?" he asked the baker casually.

"Burn it," said the baker in disgust. "What can I do with it? Who's going to eat it, I ask you? People like you, maybe, but you've got to be pretty hungry."

"Is it like this every day?" Mr Bass was hopeful.

"Sometimes it's more, sometimes it's less, usually more. It's the fault of this damn oven," said the baker, kicking it on its aluminium face. "The back ones, unless I catch them in time, they always get it. But I can't do everything myself. Look, they'll be burning now, and here I am standing talking to you." The baker obviously did not like himself at all. Even as he drew the honey-brown crisp loaves out of the oven, proof of his skill, he liked himself none the more. "Now look at the back ones," he said, almost to himself. "Bet you they're burnt already." He drew the tray forward a little and took out two loaves from the back. To his disappointment they were beautifully bronzed without a trace of burn on either side. "Well, that doesn't happen very often," he explained to Mr Bass, feeling he had let him down. "That bin's always full anyway. Night and day they get burnt."

"I can use them," said Sid suddenly. "How much d'you want for them? I mean, you won't want much for them, will you? Not if you're going to burn them anyway."

In his growing hatred for himself, the baker deliberately bit his tongue for its foolishness. "What are you going to do with them?" he parried. "No good to anybody."

"I like them," said Sid. "Any hungry man'll eat them."

The baker was suspicious, but they settled on a price. Sid arranged to call each morning for his supplies. "Now don't you be getting too careful," he called to the baker as he went off with his tray to earn the first down payment.

That chance meeting in the baker's shop that morning saw the beginnings of a revolution in the simple orthodox economy of the town. Sid set up in the business of Cut Price. From bread he went to butter and jam, and over the years to every edible commodity, until he had a chain of cut-price shops throughout the town. The small grocers trembled if a shop was for sale in their area, and at Sid's approach many closed down in anticipation of bankruptcy. Others struggled for a while and watched their years-loyal clientele slink into the King of the Crusts shops, as they came to be called, drawn by the cut prices. Legally, they had no fight against Sid. His prices, he claimed, were due to the fact that his stocks had been slightly damaged in warehouse fires, and there always seemed to be enough fires to keep him in business. Later on he went into property, and offered cheaper rents to his tenants if they worked for him. So the home went with the job, and with the job, a pension. And so he built an empire on blackmail, feared and hated by everybody.

The newspapers never missed an opportunity to hit out at him. As a consequence, he kept himself out of the public eye. But news of his re-marriage somehow leaked out, and the press decided to go to town on it. They knew that the wedding was to be a strictly family affair and very quiet, but this news was not official. And so in their announcement the day before the wedding, they hinted at rumours of vast crowds turning out to witness the new Queen of the Crusts. There had been rumours too, they said, of special police, in readiness to control the crowds that were anticipated. When their readers read what was expected of them, they hastened on the following day to oblige. The police too stood in readiness for a duty that the press had forced on them.

The Sperber family drove to the synagogue, and, as

the car approached the gates, the crowds reluctantly gave way. Sid was already there, impatient and furious.

"You had to go and open your big mouth," he said to the first Sperber jaw that presented itself.

It happened to belong to Sol, who was in no mood to be tampered with.

"Yes," he said, "that's right. I'm so proud of you, you lout, I invited the whole bloody town to your coronation."

A roar of cheers and applause from the street drowned Sol's curses. Gladys' car was approaching the synagogue. A muted chorus of, "For she's a jolly good fellow", seemed to be aware of and acknowledge her courage, while a few children in the front feebly waved a frayed Union Jack that had seen better days.

"Smile at them, Gladys," said Mrs Sperber, who refused to accept the situation as a humiliating one. Gladys waved her hand, but she could see nothing to smile about. Benny was at the synagogue door to meet the car. Gladys was the eldest of the children. She must be sixty, he thought, and as he looked at her white dress, he was filled with sadness for her. He took her arm gently and led her up the aisle. "Everything'll be all right," he whispered. "I'm going to look after you."

The synagogue was empty but for the family and the officials. It took two Rabbis to marry them, because each party belonged to a different synagogue, and besides, there was Mottel, who in spite of his recent encounter with Sid, was not to be kept out of the pulpit. While the service was intoned under the bridal canopy, Mottel stood in his box on the side, viewing the endless rows of empty benches and filling them with praying-shawls and prayer-books.

"We have from the Old Testament," he began, as soon as the ceremony was over, "a very interesting word. That word is helpmate. Now it is extremely interesting to notice that this word is a mistake. It is the translation that is at fault." The bridal party were already walking down the aisle and when the door finally closed behind them Mottel came to his point. "What the Hebrew says of Adam," he explained to the empty seats, "is, 'And God sought a help, comma, meet for him. Suitable for him.'" Mottel bowed and made his way out of the synagogue. "A help, meet for him," he murmured, as he went. "God is very clever."

As the couple walked towards their car, the crowds surged forward. Handfuls of breadcrumbs were hurled at them and some made their way down Sid's neck. Infuriated, he dragged Gladys into the car and ordered the driver to drive off. The crowds pelted the window-frames with what was left of their crumb-confetti, and, having exhausted themselves with cheers and singing, they drifted away, aimlessly, while a swarm of birds, chirping hosannas, settled on the roof of the synagogue.

5 They drove through the streets silently. Once he squeezed her hand, spreading his fat fingers round her knuckles, wriggling his palm until the pressure was even and then he withdrew his hand and put it in his

157

pocket. The gesture had been his rubber stamp on the marriage. He called to the chauffeur to stop outside one of his shops, saying he wanted to pick up some groceries. He told Gladys to go on home, where later he would join her. Gladys was not surprised at this arrangement. She was too excited over her new status to question anything. As the chauffeur turned off the side street into the main road of the town, she took off her veil. It had begun to rain, slightly at first, but by the time she reached her new home there was a steady and heavy downpour. When the car came to a stop, the chauffeur did not move. He adjusted his mirror so that he could watch Gladys, who was looking about her helplessly. She waited for a while watching his motionless back.

"Would it be too much trouble to ask you to open the door for me?" she asked.

"No trouble at all, lady," he said, opening his own door and slipping his hand on to the back handle without moving from his seat. The door sprung open and the rain drove through the car. "Better make it quick, lady," he said. "You'll get soaked if you sit there much longer."

Gladys wrapped her long dress round her knees and decided it would be easier to wear the veil than to carry it. She tied it around her head like a kerchief, stepped gingerly out of the car and rushed up the front steps to the house. "You might have shut the door, lady," the chauffeur shouted after her. "No need for both of us to get wet." But Gladys did not hear him. She was too preoccupied with manoeuvring herself up the steps. Panting, she reached the front door. She dropped the screwed-up knot of her dress and fumbled automatically in her bag. The rain beat down on her neck, for there was no shelter at the door except for some overhanging shrub with scanty foliage. It was then she realized that she had no key. She turned round and saw the chauffeur still sitting in the car outside. He smiled at her, waved his hand and drove off. There was nothing she could do. So she waited, wet and unquestioning, until Sid's car drew up outside the house.

The car door opened and a pointed umbrella shot out, opening itself slowly like a parachute. Sid ducked underneath it and, holding it well in front of him, he trudged up the steps. "Come on in," he said to Gladys as he opened the front door. "You'll get wet if you stand out there much longer."

Gladys knew the house. She had been there before, but only once after Mrs Bass' funeral. A handful of friends had come back from the cemetery to commiserate with Mr Bass. He had not made them welcome. He did not want their sympathy. He had kept them standing in the hall until they were forced to go. Gladys looked again at the closed doors of the rooms that flanked the hall. This time she was not curious about what was inside them. It was all hers now, and there was time.

"Go into the kitchen," said Sid, "and dry off. Straight through," he added. "I'm going upstairs to change."

Gladys dragged her train into the kitchen. There had been a fire, but it had gone out. A pile of wood and a bucket of coal stood in the grate. The room was cold, and smelled of closed windows and drying tea-cloths. Once again, she tied the train around her knees and arranged the fire. When it was burning, she turned around and spread herself pegless in front of it. The heat of the flames caught her legs and left her shoulders shivering. Steam rose from her shoes and a slight smell of singed leather varied the overall mustiness.

On the table was a lace cloth, torn in places and obviously demoted from the sitting-room. The sideboard was covered with large framed photographs with small seaside snaps stuck into the corner of the gilded frames. The centrepiece was a wedding group and, from where she stood, Gladys could recognize Ena Bass as a bride. Sid stood by her side, and they were flanked by in-laws in descending order of rank. A couple of brides-maids trailed down the line, and half a page-boy, whose completion lay under a view from Brighton Pier. On the end of the sideboard was a picture of a young girl in cap and gown and with best wishes. His daughter. On the other end a fat naked baby lay on its stomach on a white wool rug.

She heard Sid coming down the stairs. She dropped her spread-eagled arms and sat down, hearing the wet silk of her dress adhere to the leather chair. Sid was cheerful. He was rubbing his hands together as if he had settled a deal. He went over to her and kissed her hair. At the same time, he threw a piece of notepaper on to the table.

" I've written it all down," he said, " so as you won't forget."

The paper had a heavily printed business heading, with the title, "Credit King of the Crusts". In the place reserved for the itemized invoice, Sid had listed his instructions. "Two injections to be given twice daily. Number 1 at 9 a.m. and Number 2 at 4 p.m. Size 16 needle to be used for both." Underneath, heavily underlined and in inverted commas as acknowledgment to another source, was written, "'*It is dangerous to exceed the stated dose.*'"

"What's this for?" said Gladys.

"It's my diabetes. Had it for years," he laughed. "Just call me sugar. That'll remind you about the injections. Now what about a honeymoon?"

Since early that morning, Gladys' sense of reality had slowly ebbed from her. Nothing any longer surprised her and the core of happiness inside her was strong enough to accommodate any new suggestion or situation without questioning. Sid went over to the sideboard drawer and took out a sheaf of holiday brochures. He threw them on the table. Pictures of dazzling red suns, golden beaches, the architecture of a city, slopes of snow-covered mountains.

"Take your choice," he said. "You can lie in the sun or ski on a mountain or walk round a town. Speaking for myself, I don't like it when it's hot, I can't ski, and I don't like walking."

"What do you want to do?" Gladys asked, unwilling to take the decision.

"There's this of course." Sid dealt his trump. He threw a multi-coloured folder advertising a Mediterranean cruise on to the table. "This way, you get a bit of everything," he said. "There's a boat leaving next week. We could get on that." So it was decided. A Mediterranean cruise.

Gladys had no need to pack. The clothes she had brought from her home she left in their cases. Sid too was surprisingly packed, as if he had contemplated a voyage all his life. The cases were locked and labelled and placed in the hall a few days before their departure. Only the first-aid kit was still open, until Gladys had procured enough injections to see them through the journey. She had to go to the hospital dispensary to get the supply, because there his case was known. She sat on the long benches of the out-patients' department waiting her turn. She had tried to explain numerous times to the attendant that she did not want treatment; that she only waited for supplies. It did not matter, he had said, she would have to wait her turn with the others. Gladys took off her left-hand glove. Somehow, she felt surer of herself if her status was showing. For an hour she waited before being called to the office to register. When finally she received her prescription, she was sent to wait outside the dispensary. The ante-room to the dispensary was a long narrow corridor with a bench on one side. At the end there was a little closed hatch in the wall with the curt notice, "Knock and Wait." This she did, knocking timidly at first and sitting down as she had been instructed. After a while, she knocked again, louder this time, but there was no response from the authority that lay behind, and she hurried back to her seat. Anger, impatience and the silence drove her to knock once more. She was convinced that there was no one behind that hatch, that they were all dead, poisoned by their own prescriptions. She banged on the hatch with her gloved fist and it opened suddenly so that she fell forward on to the counter. A starched dragon in spectacles stared at her and thundered, "We're busy. You're not the only one, you know." Gladys slammed down the prescription before the woman had time to close the hatch. It came down quickly, missing her fingers by inches. "Knock and Wait" it said again. And she waited. In another half hour of waiting, all thoughts were driven out of her mind except for a growing hatred of whatever lay behind that hatch. And for some unknown reason, a fear. She knocked again, timidly this time, to remind them of her presence. She could hear nothing from inside and decided to report their negligence. She walked up the corridor to go to the registry office, but returned for her bag. There on the counter, the notice was obscured by a large box with a label, "Mr Bass. The injections." Furious, Gladys stuffed the box in her bag, banged on the hatch with her umbrella and rushed away.

They left the following morning with enough supply to secure Sid's survival for fourteen days.

But they did not need it. The boat was hardly out of harbour before Sid took suddenly ill and was advised to be landed. The unopened cases came ashore with Sid on a stretcher and Gladys following, still completely unbewildered by the turn of events. On the journey home, he recovered sufficiently to wonder whether their money would be refunded and this worry kept him awake until they reached home. They arrived late in the evening and were surprised to see, when their car drew up at the house, that the lights of the front rooms and the hall were burning. It did not occur to them that anyone was in the house and Sid immediately accused Gladys of having left them on. "It's a good job I was taken ill," he said. But the explanation met them on the front doorstep, Mrs Sperber, smiling and embarrassed.

"I thought I'd like a change for a while. O my God, what's happened?" she said, trying to apologize for her presence and express concern for Sid's state at the same time.

"What you doing here?" Sid yelled at her as he was carried through the door. "I won't be moved another step until I know. Put me down here." The carriers lowered the stretcher and looked at Gladys for instructions.

"You can go," she said. "I'll manage from here."

The two men hesitated before leaving.

"They want a tip," Sid shouted. "Give them something."

One of the carriers was carrying Sid's coat. She took it from him and felt in the pockets. They were empty. "Where's your bag, Mama?" said Gladys.

"I haven't small enough change."

"You never have," said Gladys, forced to look in her own bag. She gave them sixpence each. The men stared at each other, shrugged their shoulders and returned the money silently. The door closed behind them and the three were alone.

"Well?" Sid was prepared to let her have her say. Mrs Sperber decided to attack first.

"Well, what's so terrible about my being here? Gladys is my daughter, isn't she?" The fact was undeniable.

"Yes, that's right," Sid said, settling back on his pillow, having suddenly decided that there was no point in arguing.

"Well, aren't you going to say something?" said Gladys. Suddenly she realized she had had peace long enough. There had not been a good family quarrel for a long time. "She's got no right here. Tell her so. You didn't marry her, did you?"

"Well, ask her," said Sid. "She ought to know. She knows everything."

"She's ruled my life long enough. Now I'm free. I'm married. I've got my own home. She's got to learn to let go."

"Well, tell her," said Sid with a smile. "She's your mother, isn't she? Daughters should tell their mothers everything."

"But it's your house as well. Why don't you stand up for your rights? You coward!"

Sid was roused at last. He raised himself on one elbow.

"You big fat slut!" he frothed at Gladys. "You're no better than the last one. All the same. All you want is your rights. What the hell did I want to go and do it again for? I haven't learned my lesson. Mad I am. A housekeeper would have been a lot cheaper."

"And that's just what Gladys is," said Mrs Sperber.

Her voice came as a surprise. Gladys and Sid had forgotten she was there, and she felt she had been forgotten too. "I told you that's what he wanted you for," she added. "I warned you against him. You can scrub floors at home. But no. You've got to get married to do it. And to him." She measured the prostrate figure on the stretcher with contempt. "A nurse too, he's got. All for free. And your poor mother comes to tidy up a bit for you and get the house ready and nice for you to come back to and he's got the nerve to ask why I'm here." It was her election speech and Gladys was won over.

"Well, what d'you expect from him?" said Gladys. "Gratitude? Him? He never said thank you for anything."

It must have been the accumulation of provocation that gave Sid his sudden strength. He threw the blanket that was covering him to one side and manoeuvred himself into a standing position. A man on his back, he realized, was in no position to retaliate. He moved over to Mrs Sperber, so that his face almost touched hers, and, pointing his finger to the front door, he said, "I'm giving you five minutes to get out or I'm calling the police. As for you," he turned to Gladys, "you can go with her or you can stay, but if you go now, you're not coming back." Gladys had hoped that the row would not end in an ultimatum. It put an end to the quarrel and quarrels were made to last, to nag, to niggle into one's life like a sore that never heals. If she were home now with her mother, there were quarrels enough for a lifetime, and staying here would mean a continual threat of peace.

"Who'll give you your injections?"

"I managed before. I'll manage again."

"You'd better go," Gladys told her mother. "I'll stay here."

"You're making a mistake, Gladys, a big mistake. Well, my door will always be open. You've got a good mother."

Mrs Sperber packed her clothes quietly. She always took care to create a genuine atmosphere for her martyrdom, whenever it was called for, and silence was part of the build-up.

Gladys started to help Sid to his room. The two parties crossed on the stairs silently, and when Mrs Sperber reached the bottom she put down her case and called back to Gladys, "Don't forget," she said, "my door's always open." She waited for some reaction, but Gladys said nothing. She only grunted at the strain of dragging Sid into the bedroom. She waited impatiently to hear the closing of the front door, so that she would know that her mother had gone. She dragged Sid on to the bed and started to undress him. One side of the bed sagged with his weight and she had to lean over the other side to stop him from rolling off. She managed to get him under the blankets with one leg exposed to the needle.

"I feel ill, Gladys," he said.

"You'll feel better after your injection. Lie still. You've had an upset." She suddenly felt very tender towards him. "Soon you'll be up and well again and we'll finish our honeymoon."

"In hell, maybe," he muttered.

She plunged the needle into his thigh, inflicting more pain than was necessary. He groaned a little, twisted his mouth and opened it to let out the snore. And it remained open all night, while she sat by his side. The windows were shut and the room was stuffy, but she was afraid to open them for fear of waking him. He always shouted at her if he was woken. "Mama's right," she thought. "He treats me like a servant. Always will. That's what he wanted. In the morning maybe, he'll be dead. I'll throw away all these needles. I'll sort his clothes. I ought to get quite a bit for his new brown suit. I could give it to Sol, of course. It would fit Sol, and his shirts and things. But Sol's never been grateful. Better to give it to the old-age home. That's a bit of a waste, isn't it? He only wore it once. On to the ship. We'll get our money back, I hope. That, and the insurance and the car. That'll fetch something. And the house and the furniture; there's the washing-machine and the telly. His sister will be after it, but it's on my name. I'll ring her up and tell him and she'll say ·I did it with the injections. Mrs Schnitter will be there. I haven't seen her for a long time. She'll wear that funeral hat of hers, and I'll wear my black too, and we'll all come back here and we'll have a good cry with me in the middle."

Suddenly Sid's snoring stopped, and like a clock stopping in the dark, it woke him up. He turned over on the other side and took up the tune once more. His awakening had broken Gladys' train of thought and she was irritated. She tried hard to recapture it, but she no longer had any idea at all of what had been in her mind, like a dream that melts on waking. The room was getting more and more stuffy, and she went over to open the window. She had forgotten that the sash-cord was broken, and the window fell shut with a loud bang. Sid did not stir and the rhythm of his snoring did not change. Gladys sat down again, drawing her chair closer to the bed and watching him. He was ugly without his teeth and with his mouth open, showing his shrunken gums. Poor Sid! Her mother didn't understand him. She stroked his forehead gently and as if in acknowledgment he raised his head very slowly. She saw the effort on the veins in his neck as he craned it as if looking for something. "The wall's too high," he mumbled.

"What wall?" Gladys whispered. Sid did not answer. He lifted his head until the top of his skull lay on the pillow and his neck was arched like an old haggard swan. "It's too high," he mumbled again.

"What's too high?" Gladys was frightened. "For God's sake," she screamed at him, "what wall are you talking about?" It seemed that Sid could arch his head no higher, but the vein in his neck throbbed again with the effort, and this time his voice was very clear.

"I've got to see over the wall. My ball's gone over the wall."

Gladys began to cry. She took his head in her hands and tried to rest it flat on the pillow, but, with a sudden strength, Sid tore his head out of her grip. He twitched impotently as if his nerves were itching, and he stretched his whole body until the top of his skull touched the wicker head-board of the bed. The open mouth curled closed into a smile and his eyes opened wide and the room was filled with the fading echo of his snoring.

> And dead he lies,
> In bed he dies,
> Put a shilling in the meter
> And a penny on his eyes.

Gladys remembered the rhyme that she and her friends used to scream through the letter-box of the old undertaker's shop on their way home from school. And at the same time she remembered the washing machine and the telly and his sister and Mrs Schnitter, and she ran from the room and shut the door on the fear.

Put a shilling in the meter and a penny on his eyes. She remembered that she had not closed them, that she had left them staring over that wall with the windows and the doors and the mouth and everything else shut. She hoped that they would close of their own accord, for she dared not go in the room again. She thought of the lid of the piano in her old home which always fell to if there was a vibration in the room, so she rattled the door behind her frantically. She tried to move, but couldn't, knowing that the more space she put between her and it, the greater the fear. If she went down the stairs to the telephone all the area she encompassed would be infected by the fear. The whole house and everything in it would catch it and who would want his suit then, and the shirts and socks, even for nothing? The telephone rang, but she stood unable to move, listening to the insistent ringing, with her hands behind her holding on to the handle of the door. It was early in the morning. It must be her mother, who since Gladys' marriage had never allowed her daughter's day to begin, without her sanction on the telephone. She didn't want the ringing to stop. It was something in the house with her. If she answered it, she would have to talk to someone who wasn't there. But the bell clicked with a shrug, and fell silent and again she was alone. She edged slowly along the landing wall. It was down her back she felt the hollow, and as long as it was lined she felt secure. But there was a space between the landing and the beginning of the stairs which offered no cover. When she reached it, she twisted her arm behind her and laid it against her back so that it lined her spine, and went as quickly as she could down the stairs to the telephone in the hall. Once again she could lean against a wall and block the stare that she had left open in the room upstairs.

As she dialled her mother's number a strange excitement made her press her back more firmly against the wall. Mrs Sperber answered immediately. She always answered immediately as she sat continually by the telephone, afraid lest it would not give her a second chance.

"That you, Gladys? I've been up for hours. Couldn't sleep. I've rung you already, but you seem to be able to sleep well enough. You changed your mind?"

"About what?"

"About coming home, of course. The door's open for you. I've said it and I say it again. Don't be proud. Open your eyes to him. He's no good. I've always said so. What you want to stay with him for? Let him get a nurse. Let him pay someone to look after him."

Gladys said nothing. She saw no reason to interrupt her mother's recital of abuse.

"Gladys?" Mrs Sperber interrupted herself. "You still there?"

"Yes."

"Well, say something. What more can I say? You're stubborn, that's your trouble. Well, my door's always open. You've treated me like a dog, but I've got broad shoulders. You can come when you like." Mrs Sperber waited. "Gladys, if you're still there, why don't you say something?"

"I'm still here."

"Well, are you coming or aren't you?"

"Perhaps."

"What d'you mean, perhaps? What did you ring for? You got anything to tell me?"

"Nothing much."

"What d'you mean, much? Gladys, you're keeping something from me. What is it?"

"Nothing." Gladys started to cry.

"Oh my God, what's happened? What's the matter with you?" said Mrs Sperber. "If it's so terrible, then why don't you come home? What's he done now?"

"Nothing. He just died, that's all."

"God rest his soul," Mrs Sperber intoned automatically.

"You'd better come at once," Gladys said.

"I'll just put on my coat. Now don't worry. I'll be there very soon. My poor Gladys."

By now, Gladys was crying uncontrollably. She slithered down on to the floor holding the wall to her back. Restlessly she rubbed her eyes along her forearm, trying to stop the tears. But on the floor she felt frightened again, so she went outside the house and leaned against the porch, waiting for her mother to come. Opposite in the park, the keeper was opening the gates. He didn't know that a man had just died in a house opposite his lodge. And the cars went by hooting their horns at the corner. Each one about his business. A ladybird had settled on the canvas of the deckchair on the porch and was feeling its way to the top. And as it grew steeper, it stopped more and more often to gain breath. And almost to the top of that great green wall until it reached the ridge and fell miles and miles into eternity.

Her mother came panting up the road, breathless, her apron-strings hanging beneath her coat. She rushed up the steps and Gladys fell into her arms.

"There now," she comforted, "it happens to us all. Let's go inside." She put her arm round Gladys' waist and steadied her through the door, and shutting it behind her she turned to face her daughter. "I wish you long life," she said.

6 "In the bedroom?" she asked. Even though he was dead, she could not bring herself to pronounce his name. Gladys nodded. "You're to come with me," she said.

"I'm not going back in that room."

"Listen, Gladys, listen to me. I know what it is. I had the same with your poor father. You've got to go back in the room and look at him and the fear will go away." She pulled the little salt-bag from out of her bodice and hung it brazenly on the outside as a challenge to the evil eye. Thus armed, she led Gladys upstairs. Gladys was no longer crying. It was a relief to share the burden of a corpse with someone else. She kept as far behind her mother as Mrs Sperber would allow, hoping that she would have closed the eyes before she would have to look at Sid again. Mrs Sperber opened the door and went in. Gladys heard her gasp. "There's no one here!" Gladys ran after her. Sid was lying there staring on the bed as she had left him. "There he is," she pointed to the bed and turned her face away.

"I can see *him* all right," said Mrs Sperber, "and by the looks of him he can see me too. But there's no one watching him." She was trembling. "The dead have power, Gladys, they must never be left alone. Not until they're in the earth. One of us must stay with him."

"Shut his eyes," said Gladys. "He can't look at God like that. Shut his eyes and I'll stay." Mrs Sperber went over to the bed and stared back at him. "I knew it would happen. I always said he'd end up like this," she said, as if the corpse had just done something highly original. She opened her salt-bag and dipped her thumbs inside. And with the grains of salt clinging to her thumbs she placed them on his lids and they closed.

"You can look now," she said, "he's ready." Gladys was standing at the window, and slowly she turned her head. "Shall I tell the doctor and get the washers?" she said.

"I'll see to that. You get out his tallis, so that it'll be ready when they come." Gladys opened the suitcase. On top of the shirts lay a new praying shawl in a cellophane wrapper. She took it out of the package. "Never been worn," she muttered. "He bought it for our honeymoon."

"Hasn't he got an old one?" asked Mrs Sperber. Her sense of economy never left her. "Seems a pity to use a brand new one now."

"It's his and he'll wear it, even to the grave. A man can only love a woman if he can be sure she'll give him a decent burial." Gladys astonished herself with such a thought. It was as if Sid had spoken through her. "Whatever else he was," she said aloud, "he did love me."

"Will you stay with him now, Gladys?"

"Yes."

Mrs Sperber took a large pink handkerchief and spread it over Sid's face. It billowed a little during the laying, and then settled, assuming the contours of his nose and jutting chin.

"You'll be all right now," she said. "I'll be back soon."

Gladys drew the chair up to the bed and sat down. Her eyes were dry now and there was no threat of tears. It was strange, she thought, that most of her life had been spent in crying, mainly for herself, and that now, in the face of a concrete loss, the tears had dried up. She was grateful for the short-lived occasional happiness he had given her and she reconstructed their happy moments together in her mind, but even these memories brought no tears. For the first time she realized that she was a widow, that up to a short while ago she held the distinction in the family of being its only spinster, and that now she was the first in the family to take on another status that was equally distinctive. It gave her a kind of superiority.

She heard someone coming up the front steps. She wanted to go to the window and look out but she was afraid to be seen. Mrs Sperber answered the door. Dr Kane looked at her and then at his feet and made a point of saying nothing. He took his cigarette out of his mouth and a small curled nail-scissors out of his pocket. Very neatly he snipped off the lighted end and placed the butt in his waistcoat pocket. He went past her and straight upstairs, as if it were a convention that the dead were always to be found on a higher level. Gladys heard the door-knob turn and she rested her chin on her hands. Mrs Sperber followed him inside and led the way to the bed as if she were some guide at an exhibition. After a moment Dr Kane pulled the handkerchief away from the face. Sid was grey now and hard, like sea-shore pebbles.

"I haven't got the certificate with me," said Dr Kane, as if he had doubted Mrs Sperber's word on the telephone. "Send someone to the surgery."

Mrs Sperber saw him to the door. On his way down the stairs, he re-lit his cigarette. He paused on the porch and, turning back, he said, "Wish her long life from me."

The washers arrived with the coffin-shaped copper bath, which they discreetly placed outside the door until Gladys could be brought downstairs. At intervals the family arrived and they assembled in the front room underneath the bedroom. Everyone who came to the house was silent. Silence was a rule of bereavement and in this case the mourners were grateful. Death was no reason to see good in a man who had been labelled a blackguard all his life. The only words that could break the rule was the wish of long life to his next-of-kin, for death was either infectious, or, to honour it, it must be survived.

Gladys sat in the middle of the circle, as a poor Jenny, while the others deposited themselves symmetrically around her. Each newcomer on arrival came first into the centre with his wish, and then retired into the widening circle. Gladys in the centre would utter a sigh, and the circle would echo it back, and there would be silence until a new visitor arrived and started the game again. And all the time there was the noise of the washing in the room above, the rumbling of the bath being dragged across the floor and the hard thud of the washers' feet.

Mrs Schnitter arrived late, carrying her ledger. Her presence at a mourning was as indispensable as the corpse. A death invariably added another client to her books, or more often reinstated the same client under another category. She pushed her way into the circle and murmured her shibboleth. As she backed out a deafening noise of the bath skidding across the floor came from the room above, and the centre light of the room shivered with the vibration.

"What ever's that?" said Mrs Schnitter, realizing what it was as soon as she had said it. After all, she had been present at enough bereavements in her time to know the sounds that attended them.

"The washers," someone said, pointlessly.

"They're nearly finished, then," said Mrs Schnitter, who from long experience knew the sound of hammer and nail. "God rest his soul," she said, having decided that now Sid was absolutely alone, he must be in God's keeping. Gladys got up and went to sit beside her. Mrs Schnitter put her arm round Gladys' shoulders. Although Gladys had finally fallen off the shelf without her help, she felt sympathetic towards her. "Have a good cry," she urged. "It'll make you feel a lot better."

The door opened quietly and the three washers came in. The leader of the team—one could only guess he was the leader because he rose above the others who stood in his shadow—the leader was Mr Porse. He had only recently arrived from London, where he had been a dry-cleaner by trade. He had retired to the provinces, and spent his time assisting at Jewish ceremonies, either as a watcher of the dead, or a washer of same, or a registrar of births and marriages. His assistants were not regulars and did not share his enjoyment of their duties, though all three gave their services without payment and through sheer piety.

"It's all done," the leader bellowed, rubbing his

hands with pride of his craft, "and I wish you long life." He addressed the whole assembly. To him a death bereaved all, and a small part of every man had died in the corpse upstairs.

"Was everything all right?" Mrs Sperber whispered to him. She should have known better than to ask. Mr Porse was not famed for his tact and he sat himself down next to Mrs Sperber and, flanked by his attendants, he proceeded to give a detailed account of his job.

"Everything's all right," he started. " 'E's washed, 'e's shrouded, 'e's tallissed, and 'e's got 'is little bit of Israeli earth. Always keep a bit by me," he offered as an aside, slipping his podgy hand into his hip pocket. " 'E's done up beautiful."

"Can we see him?" Sol wanted proof.

"No," said Mr Porse sadly. "We nailed 'im down. Blood vessel burst, see. 'Ad to stuff it up with wood. Made a nice neat little wedge. A lovely job. A rabbi couldn't 'ave been served better." Gladys started to cry audibly and Mr Porse warmed to her reaction. "Well," he said, looking round him, "it 'appens every day, doesn't it, otherwise we wouldn't live, would we?" Mr Porse was becoming chatty again. "Did one only yesterday. All dolled up, 'e was. Then they decided to 'ave a post. Post mortem," he added, for the benefit of the layman. " 'Ad to do 'im up again. What a job!"

One of his assistants coughed. He knew Mr Porse to have a fund of corpse stories, each one grimmer than the last.

"Everything's all right," he said gently. "The house will be quiet now."

Mr Porse immediately misunderstood him. "It'll be quiet all right," he said, "without a man around, especially Sid." Mr Porse was obviously too familiar with death to have much respect for it when it called. "D'you remember Mr Fanish?" he asked his assistant. "You were in on 'im."

The little man preferred to forget it. The story of Mr Fanish's last rinse had been told and exaggerated beyond recognition at every subsequent bereavement. He managed to nudge Mr Porse, who grievously took the hint and, out of pique, launched into another story that his assistant had not yet heard.

"And of course," he said, "there was that terrible story about Mr Samuel. You don't know this one," he turned triumphantly to his assistant. "This one was in London," he added proudly, so that no one could challenge the truth of the story. "Before your time, Joe," he added contemptuously. "I was called in to do a job with Sam. Good boy was Sam. Quick on the job. We always worked together. Well, we went up to the room with the paraphernalia and all. All set we were, and then I undressed 'im. Mr Samuel it was, ready for the wash. Well, I took one look at 'im and I could 'ave dropped dead. 'Come over 'ere, Sam,' I says. 'Come and 'ave a look at this one.' 'Why, what's the matter with 'im?' says Sam. 'Well, can't you see?' I says. I was flabbergasted."

"Well, so? Get on with it," said Sol, feeling guilty at listening at all, yet wanting to hear the end of the story.

"Well, I looked at 'im again, and I looked at Sam,

and Sam says to me, 'What's the matter?' 'e says, 'Looks all right to me.' 'All right?' I says. 'Look at 'im.' Excuse me, ladies." Mr Porse laid his hand on his mouth and sieved his words through his fingers. "'Look at 'im, Sam,' I says, ''e's not one of ours. We got the wrong lot 'ere, Sam.' 'You're right and all,' says Sam, and 'e looks again. 'You're right. One of theirs, 'e is, all right.' 'Well, what d'you know?' I says. 'Mr Samuel, a respectable man in the community. It takes a thing like death, doesn't it, to show you what a man is? What'll we do?' I says to Sam. 'Well, we can't do it, can we?' says Sam. 'It's against the Law.' Well, we couldn't *not* do it, seeing 'as we 'ad the paraphernalia and all up there. So me and Sam 'ad a conference and we decided on a compromise. We'd wash 'im all right. We'd wash 'im good and proper, but we'd leave that bit alone. Excuse me, ladies," he said again. "And we did. We washed 'im, all but that bit. It takes a thing like Death, I say, to show you what a man really is."

Mr Porse's assistant winced. The story of Mr Fanish would have been a better choice. He dreaded any further unfolding of Mr Porse's unlimited repertoire. "We'd better go," he said.

"Why?" said Mr Porse, feeling he was just getting into his stride.

"We've got another job."

"Who? Who?" came a chorus from the mourners.

"Someone in the old-aged home."

The old-aged home was a building on the end of the town that housed anonymity. A death there was of no interest to anybody.

"Well, we'd better get on with it," said Mr Porse, rising. "We've 'ad a week with no work and now there's two in one day. It's infectious. A long life to you all," he said again, and pushed his assistants before him out of the room.

Mr Porse had broken the ice, and it was now in order for the mourners to indulge in conversation. They started with neutral subjects like the weather, in which everybody participated and, as the topic exhausted itself, people split off into little groups. Mrs Schnitter probed Mrs Sperber for details of the death, while the men huddled together organizing the rota for the watch. Mottel was stubbornly refusing to take a turn. The rest of the family sat together and discussed Gladys' future, while Gladys sat alone. There was a terrible sadness on her face as she looked at those around her. She knew the shallowness of their concern, that for most of them this was a social visit with a good excuse and for her family it was a time for speculation. But upstairs he was alone too, and nobody really cared. And the sense of his isolation and her own bound her to him, and perhaps for the first time she truly loved him. She got up and made for the door. Nobody noticed her leave the room, and conversation continued in a guilty undertone, the women whispering to each other to lend mystery to mundane things.

Gladys walked upstairs into the bedroom with no fear. The bedclothes were neatly rolled back and the coffin rested on two trestles by the side of the bed. It was covered with a dark blue cloth, with a gold-embossed shield of David in the centre. A coil of thick rope lay underneath one of the trestles. A short time ago, she thought, the room had looked so different. Through the new smells of carbolic and deal, there seeped the familiars of antiseptics and coated tongues. She wanted him back. It's not fair, she thought. Now I could really love him. "I love you, Sid," she wept on to the cloth, "but it's not poor Gladys, it's not poor anybody, it's poor Sid. He's gone," she said, trying to convince herself, "and to-morrow he'll be in the earth, and the room will be a visitor's room because of the fear, and because they won't stay for long. It's wrong," she whispered, "he didn't deserve to die, not if I could love him." And she laid her head on the coffin and wept like a child.

Sol came in silently. He put his arm round her shoulders.

"Don't stay up here, Gladys," he said gently. "It'll upset you all the more. Go down with the others."

"It's my sorrow," she said. "No one else's. It's mine. I can't share it with anybody." She looked up at Sol. Her hair straggled over her eyes and the grey strands were darker with the moisture. Tears wrinkled down her cheeks. "What will become of me?" she said.

"God looks after widows and orphans," said Sol. He spoke as if from personal experience. "And you're a real widow, Gladys," he said gruffly, realizing her sorrow. "And God knows a fake when he sees one."

When Gladys was gone he sat down, shoved his little black cap to the back of his head and let the tears flow freely. His father was in that box, his wife and his children. He dragged his wounded arm across his eyes and sniffed loudly. "A lot of rubbish," he said to himself, and forced a smile to his mouth. An hour to go, a whole hour without a smoke. He leaned back in his chair and with his feet he played with the thick coil of rope.

Jewish dead are not trusted to hang about too long, so they are buried quickly. Sid was to be buried the following day. The family sat around Gladys or went up on the watch, or made tea or conversation while the day rolled into night and the following morning. The front door was left open; women who had come to commiserate came inside, leaving their menfolk in their cars waiting to follow the hearse. Gladys had spent most of the waiting time with Sid. Two other watchers were there with her, and as the hour of the funeral approached the watch was reinforced as if the power of the dead grew stronger on the brink of the grave. Then suddenly as if a sign had been given them, the watchers filed out and Mrs Volpert, the wife of one of the town's ministers, came into the room and up to the coffin where Gladys stood. She rested her handbag on the wooden box and took out a pair of scissors. With these she split the lapel of Gladys' woollen cardigan, and the black stitches dropped like tears. Then she led Gladys out of the room, past the four pallbearers waiting outside and down the stairs, into the hall where the women were waiting.

She stood among them, her eyes riveted to the top of the stairs. They heard movement on the landing, and at the bend the first bearer came into sight. They were moving very slowly and obviously had difficulty in negotiating the turning on to the stairway. The fourth pallbearer was a good deal shorter than the other three, so that the coffin lolled sideways like a table with a short leg. The short man had tried to remedy the deficiency by placing his hand on his shoulder under the box as a wedge. But this did not seem to help matters and the sorrow of the mourners downstairs was sharpened by the excitement of the possibility that the coffin's last passage would be a rough one. There was much manoeuvring and shifting before the cortège came into the straight, but their difficulties were by no means over. The shorter member of the quartet had stupidly been placed in the front where the maintenance of balance depended. They shuffled down two steps and at each move the coffin slid forward. On the third step the short man decided not to descend, so that the height of the stair would compensate for his lack of inches. This time the coffin rocked to the other side and the cortège began to look like a drunken carnival. Somehow they managed to reach the bottom of the stairs, where others stood ready to help them. The mourners crowded round the front door and watched the coffin slide into the hearse. The procession of cars moved slowly down the road and they watched it out of sight to the last car. And then the mourning started in earnest.

It lasted a week. The low mourning stool, the candles, the visitors, the prayers. During the week, Gladys, as chief mourner, assumed a kind of majesty. Each day the women came to serve her, with basinfuls of food and well-worn platitudes, which tided them through their stay. And there were the long silences after the nightly prayers, when the women sat with their legs ajar and the candle burnt in the glass.

As the week passed, the visits became less formal, and people began to speak about things other than the inevitability of Death and the healing powers of Time. Widow's Wednesday marked the turning point in the tenor of mourning. The women of the community who had already been widowed coincidentally arrived on the same day. Widows of long standing showed a slight contempt for the novitiate. " It's not so bad in the beginning," they said, " when people come to see you, but you wait with the years and people forget. Diabetes, was it? Mine had it. Sugar's a sly one, sugar is. What needle did you use?"

" Make the best of it," said one, and " Make the most of it," another.

Throughout the week Mrs Sperber acted as a guardian and general hostess. She was queen of the widows anyway, and although she was not entitled to sit on a low stool, she assumed all the attributes of chief mourner. Lately she had taken to fingering her clothes, making a fold in her dress between the thumb and forefinger, and rubbing them together as if sampling the material, fingering all over her body as if to assure herself of her being.

In the evening the men came in for prayers. When the quota of ten had been gathered, Mottel's high-pitched call to draw the Lord's attention would start them off, and they would race through the incantations until all had been flagged down.

And when night came, the room was empty, with the heavy scent of flowers, with the stool and Gladys in the middle, and the glass with the ever-lit candle, that had burned a yellow chrysanthemum black.

PART V

1 What Sid had had in his life, and had for a short while been able to share with Gladys, did not belong to him anyway. While his first wife was alive, he had, for tax purposes, transferred most of his assets to her name, and in her will she had left everything to her sister. Even the house in which they had lived, they were furnished tenants of, and, when Sid died, Gladys was left with nothing. Daily the house was denuded of its furnishings. She never went out for fear that she would find the doors locked on her return and the house requisitioned during her absence. She still had a telephone, the television, and the bedroom was complete. For some reason, the drawing-room furniture had been left with the old grand piano that had never been played on, on the carpetless floor. With these amenities, she could live on indefinitely. Until one day the solicitor's letter came and the notice to quit. It was still very early when the letter arrived, but there no longer seemed any point in staying in a house which had been taken from you. In some ways she was glad to be relieved of her guard and she dressed quickly and left the house.

The streets were quiet at this hour with the last echo of early morning workers and trams. The shutters were going up on the fish market, and shoals of bright silver fish were flung on to the marble slabs, still wriggling each other like young lovers until they were spent and still. Old Tom, who had been the town's tolerated tramp for as long as Gladys could remember, sat on the drawbridge of the disused castle, sharing his crust of bread with the birds. The mist lifted as Gladys reached the city bridge and leaned over the railings at the dirty water below. The steps that led down to her birthplace were still covered with last night's litter and the scum from the river where the tide had left its mark. The river was low now and not like a city river at all, and where the tide had ebbed on both banks, it had uncovered the grey, dry pimples and pockmarks of the river's skin. A line of wellingtoned children waded across the stream to the other side, collected a few stones and waded back. A woman ran down the steps towards the river. She was carrying a bucket of rubbish and was shaking a clenched fist at one of the children mid-stream. The boy attempted to retreat to the other bank, but there were others behind him precariously tottering on the single stone path. He stood for a while, with legs apart, hovering on two stones in indecision and watching his mother feed the pigswill into the muddy water. Slowly he went forward to take his punishment. An engine whistle echoed across a distant bridge taking a train away to London, away from the caged shuttered city, and the whimpering of the little boy who had to leave the flowing river behind him, and, like Gladys, was going home.

She knew the way to the house blindfold. The forty-five stone steps along the river, the one-sided street of houses, all of them numberless, exhausting the river source for their names. The parrot at "Water's Edge" that had talked to Gladys when she was a child, was stuffed now, and sat on a rack, its sad glass eyes reflecting the bars of its cage. The window with the grating at "River Brink", with a bed behind it, where once a crippled child had lain, but dead now, and the grating still there. The rusty padlock on the telephone box on the corner with no telephone inside.

She opened the gate to her mother's house and pressed the bell. She waited a long time before bending down to look through the letter-box. The hall was empty, and the doors to the adjoining rooms closed. Her mother must be out. She did not want to use her key. She had come strictly as a visitor. But it was cold and she was thirsty for a cup of hot tea. She felt her key in her handbag and dropped it back into her purse. She was angry. Her mother had no right to be out. She ought to be expecting her. The door should be wide open to welcome her back. Suddenly she heard footsteps on the stairs inside. Mrs Sperber was just getting up. The footsteps grew louder and more hurried and suddenly the door was opened wide and a scream of joy and welcome broke through Gladys' irritation. "You're home," cried Mrs Sperber, triumphant, wiping away a tear with the belt of her dressing-gown. "What did I always say? My door's always open."

Gladys was immediately on her guard. "I've come for a visit," she said decidedly. Mrs Sperber laughed, and her laughter drove through Gladys like a sword. "I'm not staying," she added defiantly, "I've got a home of my own to go to." As she said it, she saw the empty rooms, the dead telephone, the solicitor's letter.

"Your bed's made up," Mrs Sperber persisted.

"I've got my own bed," Gladys countered, weakening.

"So have your own bed. Stubborn as ever. Come in, anyway, if that's not too much to ask. I don't suppose you'd say no to a cup of tea."

She led Gladys into the kitchen, and they took up their old positions round the table. The crumbs from last night's supper still lay on the tablecloth, the dead fire in the morning grate, and the grandfather clock that had ticked Sid away. Gladys shifted uncomfortably in her chair. The readjustment was too easy, the return seemed too automatic to be a return at all. As a protest, she changed her seat and sat in a chair at the end of the table, where in the old days Sol the youngest had had his place. Mrs Sperber understood the move but did not reckon with it as a major withdrawal. "I'll put the kettle on," she said. She felt that, in her absence, Gladys could adjust herself more easily.

Left alone, Gladys combed the room for a sign that something, however small, had changed. But it was not the familiarity of the battle ground that frightened her, but the unchanging face of the enemy. When Mrs Sperber returned with the tea tray, Gladys had resettled herself in her own seat. Mrs Sperber felt she had won the first round with stratagem.

Gladys felt less depressed when she had finished her breakfast. She had already decided to return to her mother the moment she had left the requisitioned house on the other side of the town. And having taken the decision, she was now beginning to see its advantages. She had her own furniture, or part of it, the luxuries of a television and washing machine were hers, which in her generosity she would share with her mother. "She's an old woman," she thought, watching her finger the cloth of her dressing-gown. "She can't have much longer to go, and then this house at least will be mine. I shan't have scrubbed its floors for fifty years for nothing." The tenderness she felt for the floors and the furniture was far greater than any feelings she might have for the people who used them. She no longer wanted the house for its memories or associations, but for the tiled floor in the hall, the loose brick in the landing alcove and the flaked parched wood on the window frames.

They discussed her future amicably. Gladys was to move her furniture in the next day. She was to share the bedroom with her mother as she always had, but for the short interval of her marriage, since Mr Sperber had died. Gladys did not object to this last suggestion. She would sleep in her mother's room as a concession, as an excuse to look after her, but she insisted on having her own sitting-room, housing within its damp flowered walls the elegant drawing-room furniture and her television, her own room, in which her mother would always be welcome as a guest. It seemed a reasonable arrangement and both women, for their own reasons, were happy about it. "Let her have her own room," Mrs Sperber thought. "She'll feel independent that way, as long as she comes back at night, like in the old days."

The whole day passed pleasantly. Gladys made the

fire and her mother prepared the day's food. Together they went through the rooms of the house, deciding the new positions of the furniture. It was like a game in which the competitors had opposing ideas of the prize, but they played none the less, each politely keeping to her own tracks. And when the family gathered in the evening to celebrate Gladys' homecoming, they drank a toast to the health of the two women, not knowing that they were drinking to the ruin of one of them.

2 The following day a great van drew up outside the house. The children of the neighbourhood gathered round. Furniture vans were big, like hearses. But arrival or departure, they spelled change, new faces, new manners, a threat to the *status quo*. They crowded round the tail of the van, watching the men slide a Queen Anne dressing-table down the ramp, their little faces clouded with hostile curiosity. Mrs Sperber was at the door, directing operations. It was a role given her by Gladys, who was herself upstairs giving the final orders for placing. The transference of Gladys' home took the whole morning, but the children did not disperse. Occasionally one or two would leave the crowd and return, reinforced by their gang. There were countless offers of help, which the removers disdainfully declined as if their skill had been cast in doubt. The elegant pieces of furniture, the cheval mirrors, the gilt inlaid bed with the pink satin counterpane, the black

grand piano with the brass candlesticks soldered to the fretted woodwork, the ladderback chairs, the dazzling chandelier. "Must be a duchess," said one little boy, to whom whoever the owner of the furniture turned out to be would be a duchess for ever. "A duchess living here down by the river," said another little boy who, in his twelve years by the riverside, had come to know disenchantment. "Maybe it's stolen property," volunteered another boy. This suggestion appealed to his gang, who, in view of the contrast between the goods and the neighbourhood, thought it quite feasible. With individual comments and contributions, they convinced themselves that this was so and set out to convert the rest of the children who were still undecided. When the last article was carried out of the van, a small jewel cabinet, embossed with mother of pearl that needed four men to carry, their suspicions were confirmed and they withdrew to the corner of the street in a huddle of conspiracy, leaving one little boy, hogging the jewel case with his eyes, and knowing that his fairy godmother was inside the box.

The door of the house closed and the van drove away and everything was the same again, except for a gang of boys on the corner who had already forgotten why they were there.

Inside the house Mrs Sperber had joined Gladys in the bedroom. From the door they surveyed the jumble of furniture inside. It was already quite clear that one of the property owners would have to withdraw. To get into a bed, one would have had to leap two wardrobes and squeeze behind a chest of drawers. From the doorway the room looked like a store-house for selection for an auction sale. The long mirror of a Victorian dressing-table reflected a svelte Edwardian bedroom chair, turned sideways as if insulted at the contact. Gladys' inlaid bedstead leaned reluctantly on the brass back of her mother's bed, which she remembered lying in as a child.

The two women looked at each other silently, ready to do battle.

"There's not enough room," said Mrs Sperber superfluously. "Some of it will have to go."

"Whose?" they asked together.

"I've had my bedroom furniture since I was married," sobbed Mrs Sperber.

"So have I."

"Your poor father slept in that bed. I nursed all you children in it."

Gladys desperately strove for a counterpoint, and not finding one, she got angry. "Papa's dead, and the children are grown up," she said.

"D'you want my house?" Mrs Sperber asked quietly. "Take it. I'm eighty. I might live another ten years. If you can't wait, take it, take it all. Thank God I've got a home of my own to go to." She looked at Gladys' questioning face. "In here," she sobbed, beating on her forehead. "It's here, it's all here. Take the house, if that's what you're after, throw me into the street, let me go out and beg. Let them all see what you really think of your mother. Take the clothes off my back," she added as an afterthought. Mrs Sperber had a real talent for organizing her own martyrdom. In her moments of loneliness and self-pity, she had walked the streets of the town a thousand times as the shoeless castaway. She always took care to take off her shoes for this was the greatest humiliation she could endow herself with. She knew all the people she had met on her way, and had given each one the commiseration they handed out to her. She was on the end of the bridge, leaning over the parapet, when someone touched her on the shoulder. It was late and dark— Mrs Sperber always undertook her calvaries at a late hour, preferably in fog, or sometimes, to give variety, in a raging blizzard. If the latter, then she would have to accommodate bleeding feet into her story which even she found too far-fetched. She turned round and in the darkness it was difficult to recognize the woman who had touched her. But she saw the big holdall the woman carried and the ledger sticking out and knew that it was Mrs Schnitter.

"What are you doing out so late, Mrs Sperber? And all alone?" It would never occur to Mrs Sperber to ask Mrs Schnitter the same question. Bit players are on the stage solely for the sake of the protagonist.

"I've been thrown out."

"The bailiffs?"

"The bailiffs." Mrs Sperber laughed. "They're not daughters of mine. They're human. No. No bailiffs. My daughter. My own flesh and blood."

"I don't want your house," said Gladys.

Mrs Sperber was furious at Gladys' interruption of what had threatened to become one of her best scenes to date. She would have to reconstruct it at another opportunity.

"It was your idea that I should come back, don't forget," said Gladys. "If you've changed your mind, I can go and take my furniture with me."

"We'll come to some arrangement," said Mrs Sperber, suddenly reasonable, and they left the room, closing the door on the problem they had brought upon themselves.

3 There was a safe by Mrs Sperber's bed. It had been there since the beginning of her marriage, and not even during the rare redecorations had it once been moved. Behind it was the original wallpaper, of an ivy-leaf pattern, faded now and wattled with damp. The square of the floor which it occupied had sunk over the years with its weight. Throughout its existence there had been only one key, and this had belonged to Mrs Sperber. When Sol had been a boy, she had once caught him tampering with the lock and she had immediately replaced it with one of the combination locks which were then fashionable. No one knew the word-combination and on every journey that Mrs Sperber made to the safe she was seen to mutter it silently between her lips.

The safe contained all Mrs Sperber's wealth. She had a bank too but it was only a front and contained the few legitimate pounds of her various pensions and war bonds. In the safe lay Mrs Sperber's jewellery, her diamonds, her rings, watches and pearls and other valuables, together with wads of notes accrued and preserved over the two war years. Once a week, Mrs Sperber made an official journey to the safe but no one knew how often she reassured herself during her nights alone in the room. Every Friday, before the lighting of the candles, she would pick up her bag behind her on the kitchen chair and go upstairs to the bedroom, fingering the pearls round her neck and mumbling the combination on the way, like a rabbi on his way to open the Ark. Nowadays she rarely put anything inside, but she would open the safe merely to check its contents and perhaps to change the position of a thing or two. Having satisfied herself, she would come downstairs again, and, in good faith, light the Sabbath candles.

The secret of the combination she had guarded all her life. It was probably the only confidence she had ever respected, until once, in her later years, she forgot what the combination was. She had made her usual trip to the safe and found everything in order. After supper, she went to bed early because she was feeling unwell and generally miserable. She fell asleep soon enough, having induced a scene of martyrdom that had not been vivid enough to shut out reality and with the boredom of it she fell asleep and into a nightmare. Mr Sperber had come to her bedside and asked for his weekly allowance of cigarette money. "But Abel," she said gently. "You had it yesterday. To-day is only Saturday."

"To-day is Friday," he said. "You've just lit the candles."

"Then if I've lit the candles, it's already the Sabbath and I can't give you the money on the Sabbath."

"Then why didn't you give it me before you lit the candles?" he asked.

"I gave it to you," she insisted.

"Well, where is it then?" he asked. "I haven't got it You must have put it back in the safe. Go and look." He picked up his big tailoring scissors and opened them close to her eyes. He was smiling and muttering something about pleats, so she obeyed and went straight to the safe. Abel followed and she tried to keep him out of the bedroom, but he forced his way inside and stood close behind her as she bent down to the lock. And suddenly the combination word wasn't in her mind any more. She no longer had any idea after all those years of what it had been.

"I've forgotten it," she screamed in terror, knowing that he would not believe her.

"But *I* know it," he said. "I've known it all the time." He laughed, quietly at first and then louder and louder until even the safe shook with the vibration of the sound. "I know it," he laughed again, "I've known it all my life." The tears were running down his face at the thought of the deception. "And what's more," he said, pausing to get his breath, "I'm not going to tell you." He opened his scissors again and rested them on her shoulder. Then bending down he thrust his face into hers and whispered, "I'm not going to tell you."

Mrs Sperber woke suddenly, clutching her shoulder. The room was very dark and she felt her way out of the bed to put on the light, half-suspecting that she was not alone. When she reached the door, she waited for the echo of her footsteps to die away and she pressed the switch slowly as if she wanted the light to come gradually. The room was quite empty and silent. The bed looked very disturbed and unoccupied. Mrs Sperber was frightened. She had not dreamt about Abel for a long time. She had not even consciously thought of him. Her loneliness and misery had really nothing to do with his absence. She sensed the evil eye in the room and tugged at the salt-sack round her neck. Perhaps if she opened the safe it would reassure her. She went back to her bed and took her bag from under the pillow. Out of it came the bunch of keys, which she laid on the bed until she had set the combination. She kept looking behind her in fear that someone was there. And as she bent down to the lock, she realized that it was true. She had forgotten the word. Absolutely. In a rising panic, she fiddled with the lock and turned it in all directions until she realized that there were at least a thousand permutations to be tried. "Perhaps I'm still dreaming," she said, "and to-morrow I'll be able to open it." She climbed wearily to bed, half believing that she was still asleep, that the light was not really on, that the keys that had fallen on to the floor were still in her bag under her pillow, but when she woke in the morning, the naked electric bulb in the centre dazzled her and she knew now that she had really forgotten the combination.

She got up, switched off the light and dressed, not knowing what to do. She did not want to tell the children. They had often asked her to tell them the combination in case of emergency, but she had always laughed and refused. She would have to call in a lock-smith and have it forced.

When he arrived half an hour later, she led him up to the bedroom and stood behind him at the safe.

"Just force it. I'll open the door," she said.

"I think I know this lock," he said. "I'll try a few first. Perhaps we can save it after all. Ruth, was it?" he asked, looking over his shoulder.

"No. I don't remember. I don't think so."

"Town? Bird? Book? Chin?" he asked at intervals.

"No," said Mrs Sperber again, "I don't remember. Force it," she said angrily. "You can be all day trying."

He fiddled with the combination once more and turned the key in the lock. The safe slowly creaked open.

"There you are, ma'am," he said, getting up and allowing Mrs Sperber to replace him. "Abel, ma'am, that's what it was. You're getting old," he said. "Better write it down somewhere."

Now, once and for all, the safe and Mrs Sperber were a tightly closed partnership that, like a coffin, would outlive a lifetime.

This, together with the single bedstead that was its guardian, was the only piece of furniture Gladys left in the room. Her mother had gone to spend the day with Miriam, and Gladys had arranged for the removers to call soon after she was gone. For six months since the furniture had been moved in, the room had remained as it was. Every night it had been a major operation to get near the bed and another to get into it. Her mother's promises of coming to some arrangement had not materialized and, every time the matter was discussed, it always ended with Mrs Sperber voluntarily offering up her homestead, and Gladys weakly insisting that this was never her intention. All Mrs Sperber's old furniture from the bedroom had been moved on to the landing. The two workmen took off their caps and leaned against the wardrobe.

"Where now, ma'am?" they asked.

Gladys turned her back on them.

"In the cellar," she said hoarsely. "That's all they're good for."

Mr Sperber's old bed was the first to go. Gladys stood watching its descent over the balustrade. They did not handle it very gently and, as it rocked down the stairs, Gladys was reminded of Sid's coffin. She was tempted to ask them to bring it back up again. But it's not as if it's going out of the house, she thought. It'll lie here still.

"Why don't you give it away, miss?" said one of the removers, as they paused for breath at the bottom of the stairs. "I'll take it off your hands."

"Thank you," said Gladys, "but it's not mine. It's my mother's, and I think she wants to keep it." The men lifted their burden again and soon the bones of Mrs Sperber's memories lay buried in the cellar.

The rest of the furniture followed, and when the men had left Gladys shut herself in the kitchen, afraid to look at what she had done. "It's only reasonable," she kept saying to herself. "One of us had to come to an arrangement. If she makes a fuss, I'll leave." And there her thinking stopped, for there was nowhere it could go.

Mrs Sperber returned just before bedtime. She was in a strangely happy mood. Downstairs the house bore no visible signs of change and as she went into the kitchen she suggested to Gladys a cup of tea before they went to bed. Gladys wanted to have the matter out and done with it, and she was tempted to tell her mother all that had happened during the day. But perhaps on the other hand it would be better to keep her in good humour. They settled around the kitchen table. Suddenly Mrs Sperber began to laugh.

"What's so funny?" said Gladys.

"You're all waiting for me to die," Mrs Sperber said.

"What's funny about that?"

"Miriam's been nagging me all day. That's all she asked me there for. Solicitors as well. They want me to make a will. 'I don't want anything, Mama,' Miriam kept saying. 'Nobody wants anything from you, but you've got to make a will.' 'Why?' I said, 'If you don't want anything, why should I give it to you?'" Mrs Sperber was chuckling all the time and fingering the lapel of her overcoat that she had not yet taken off. "I'll have the last laugh yet," she laughed. "I've made a will all right."

"Now, Mama, you know Miriam's right. And you haven't made a will. You know you haven't."

"May the Almighty strike me dead if I'm telling a lie!"

Of late, Mrs Sperber had fallen into the habit of

205

invoking all the curses of God and Man to support the truth of everything she said. And it was at about the same time that she had fallen into the habit of feeling and testing the material of her clothes, as if on the one hand she was daring the Lord to take away her life, and clinging to it firmly on the other.

"Oh, stop cursing, Mama," Gladys said. "What does it matter, anyway? If you've made a will, well and good. If not, it's all the same. One thing's certain. You can't take it with you. Let's go to bed." Gladys let her mother pass her on the stairs. "There's a surprise waiting for you in the bedroom," she said, as jovially as she could.

"A surprise? For me?" said Mrs Sperber and she hurried to the room, pausing outside the door before opening it. "You're a good girl, Gladys," she said, as Gladys reached the top of the stairs. "Sometimes I think you're the only one who isn't panting for my death. A surprise," she whispered in anticipation and opened the door.

Gladys wished fervently that she could have the day over again. She thought of her father's bed lying in the cellar, and in the knowledge that she had done wrongly, she began to work up a feverish hatred against her mother as some kind of defence. She remembered in great detail how throughout her life her mother had thwarted her on every side, how she could never let go, and worst of all, how she, Gladys, had fallen into the habit of enjoying it. She went into the bedroom and found her mother standing between the safe and her own bed. She was looking at herself in Gladys' table mirror, questioningly, as if surprised at the change in her features, like an exile who, having known so intimately the contours of his skin, finds them taut and misshapen in an alien home. Mrs Sperber sat on the bed and hid her face in her hands.

" What's the matter? " said Gladys. " Don't you like it? "

" Like it? " said her mother, dropping her hands to her lap and refolding the pleat in her skirt. " It's lovely. It's beautiful, your furniture. But where is my home? "

" It's here, Mama, it hasn't changed."

Mrs Sperber got up. She ignored what Gladys had said.

" Where is it? " she asked again. " Where's my home? Where is my husband and where are my children? Where are my tears and where is my laughing? Where? " she thundered, crystallizing the growing list of lost property into one single image. " Where is your poor father's bed? "

" In the cellar."

" In the cellar? " cried Mrs Sperber, incredulous. " You weren't satisfied with burying him once? And why didn't you take my bed too? That's where I belong. By his side. What difference does it make if in the cellar or the earth? You're another one who can't wait. You want the house to yourself. You want to wake up in the morning and know that the day is yours, that it doesn't depend on anyone else, that you can come and go as you please."

" That would be wonderful," Gladys thought. " God knows, I've deserved some peace."

" But it won't come so soon," her mother went on,

" and till it comes you'll pay for it. Who pays the rates on this house? And pays to keep it going?"

"I'll pay rent like any other lodger," Gladys said, relieved that her mother had offered her atonement on easy payments. "I'll get a rent book to-morrow."

"And you'll pay in advance."

Gladys started to undress as a sign that the deal was settled.

"Shall I turn off the light," she said, " before I get into bed?"

"Do as you please," said Mrs Sperber. "It's your house now, you'd better start being economical. I can undress in the dark. It's not my room any more and the less I see of it, the better. A surprise," she muttered. "One of these days there'll be a surprise," she laughed. Gladys heard her fingering her keys. A flash of light from a torch flooded her corner of the bedroom. Mrs Sperber was at the safe. After the fumbling with the lock and the keys, Gladys heard the safe door creak open and her mother fiddling inside. " A surprise," she jeered again. "I'll give you surprises. One day. I'll have the last laugh yet and may the Almighty cut out my tongue if that one isn't true."

4 "May the Almighty strike me blind if I'm telling a lie," said Mrs Sperber, tightening her lips. "That's not my signature. I never signed it."

The rent book lay on the table. Almost three months had passed since Gladys had been transferred to a lodger's footing and she had paid her rent regularly. Every Friday, before the lighting of the candles, she had handed her rent book to her mother. She had written down all the particulars and all that was left was for her mother to sign. Her feeble signature, under the heading, "Collected By", straggled like a family of spiders down the length of three columns.

"That's not my writing," she suddenly exclaimed. "You've forged it. You've never given me a penny. Three months' rent," she laughed. "Where is it? Or have you hidden it somewhere? Have you got another surprise for me?"

"You've had my rent every week. Every Friday. You know you have. There's your name. I couldn't write like that. I don't know what you've done with the money. It's probably in the safe."

"You'd like to look, wouldn't you?" said Mrs Sperber. "There's time," she said, "plenty of time. But until that time, you owe me three months' rent."

It was pointless to argue. "I'm going out," said Gladys.

"And where are you going? Leaving me alone. Going to tell your friends, I suppose, that your mother's robbing you. I've got friends too. And I've got a story. Two sides to every story, you know. Where are you going?" she screamed after Gladys into the hall.

"I'm going to friends all right," Gladys said and the door slammed behind her.

Mrs Sperber picked up the rent-book and examined the signature. She took another piece of paper and wrote down her name. Then she laid the rent-book alongside the paper and compared the writing. "It *is* my writing," she said to herself after some scrutiny. "But I don't remember writing in this book at all. Maybe I did. I don't remember. But if I did," she said, reasoning to herself further, "where did I put the money?" She reached behind her for her bag and took out the keys. Slowly she climbed the stairs to her bedroom and went to the safe. She looked inside. On one side of the safe lay a pile of notes, interrupted at regular intervals by narrow gaps, like a tall, many-sandwiched cake. She took out the pile with both hands and laid it on the bed. In between each layer of pound notes, lay two half-crowns. Gladys' weekly rent. "She must have paid then," Mrs Sperber said to herself, "but I really don't remember writing my name." She took the pile of money and replaced it in the safe before locking up. "She couldn't have paid me," she said, coming down the stairs. "I don't remember signing that book. She's robbing me. She can't wait," she said, looking around the familiar room. "Even while I'm here, she can't wait, and after all I've done for her."

When Gladys had left the house, she had had no idea of where she was going. She seemed not to participate in the direction of her steps, only in so far as they took her away from her mother. From one of the houses in the street came the sound of a telephone. "Somebody wants somebody," she thought. She looked around and saw the bridge behind her in the distance and the city centre with its white civic buildings on the other side. A bus passed her and stopped by the traffic lights. She would have to wait for the bus to pass before she could cross the road. Too impatient to wait for a moment, she walked across the road until the stationary bus obstructed her and automatically she got on, settling herself on the farthest seat on the inside. The bus moved off and she was restless again. Her feet tapped impatiently on the steel ramp of the seat. The conductor came for her fare, but, having no idea where the bus was going, she asked for the terminus, not caring where it would lead her. It was a Sunday and the streets were quiet. Only a few people boarded the bus from time to time, but nobody seemed to get off. Some of them carried bunches of flowers and all of them looked very sad. An old man, carrying a silver vase, halted the bus at a request stop, but the driver sped past him, and he was left, with one foot in the gutter, shaking his vase as if it were a trophy. At last they came to the end of the line. The bus stopped, but no one seemed to be in a hurry to leave. " All change," the conductor shouted and one by one they straggled off the bus. Gladys was the last, and as she alighted, she recognized her whereabouts, though the route they had taken had seemed quite unfamiliar to her. She followed the other passengers up the hill, and when they turned off the road, she carried straight on. The Jewish cemetery was farther afield. When she reached the gates, the keeper was sitting inside his lodge. He looked surprised to see her, and pleased too, as he put the key in the gate to open it.

"It's been a long time," he said from behind the bars.

"Yes, I know."

"Haven't seen your mother around here lately, Not since poor Mr Sperber's unveiling, in fact."

"It's a bit too far for her to come nowadays. But she'll come one day, I suppose."

"She will indeed," he said. And he opened the gate to welcome her in.

Gladys walked down the path to the far end of the graveyard. She passed Sid's grave on the way, but kept her gaze fixed ahead, as if that was not what she had come for. Almost at the end of the cemetery lay a group of very old graves, their headstones crumpled to the earth they protected. The inscriptions were unreadable and covered with verdigris. This part of the cemetery was overgrown and neglected and it seemed that no one was alive to visit it any more. Gladys made for a grave on the side of the group, and sat down on a nearby headstone, looking at the unruly growth that covered it. Here lay her grandfather, the first of his family to be buried in exile. His father lay in Russia, at home, under a Yiddish inscription corroded by the snow. He had been her mother's father, and Gladys had hardly known him. But he had been her first experience of death. She remembered his funeral, the day she did not have to go to school, the men with long beards and sideboards and her mother crying. That had been the worst of it all. She picked up a pebble and threw it on the grave, and then another and another to make up for the hundreds of visits she had never paid, until she had built a pyramid of pebbles in the middle of the grave. Then, taking up a large stone, she threw it at the little structure and it fell apart, crackling down the sides. "Did you begin it all?" she whispered. She did not hear the footsteps behind her, and it was not until an old woman stood by the next grave that Gladys noticed that she was not alone. In such proximity, and with such a common purpose, a greeting was inevitable. The old woman turned to pick up a pebble and in doing so looked into Gladys' face.

"You visiting?" she said.

"My grandfather. And you?"

"My mother, God rest her soul." The old woman placed her pebble on the grave and sat on a bench alongside. "I couldn't wait to get rid of her while she was alive. She was difficult. And now she's gone, it's worse. Much worse."

"D'you come here often?"

"Every week. It's my whole life."

Gladys got up quickly and hurried away as if the woman had brought a plague with her. "I should never have come here," she thought. But she realized that she had never intended to come, neither to the cemetery, nor to her grandfather's grave, nor to that of her own father, at whose grave she now found herself standing. The double tablet of stone stood at the head, the one side blank like an unfinished commandment. She stared at her father's inscription so that it settled on to her vision to the extent that when she looked towards the white stone at its side the same inscription transferred itself on to the blank white marble, blurred now and unreadable. She picked up a pebble and put it on her father's grave but it rolled over and fell on to the earth beside. She sat down on the earth and cried. But the tears, she knew, were not for her father or her grandfather, or even for her mother, but for the little old woman at the end of the cemetery.

She heard a bell from the keeper's lodge. It was closing time. From all over the cemetery, isolated figures were taking their leave. Gladys watched them converge on the gate, where they looked like a vast crowd. She hurried towards them to find a contact with the living and she followed them down the hill to the bus stop where the strangers were already waiting.

When she got home, Mrs Sperber was waiting for her in the kitchen.

"Where have you been?" she asked as soon as Gladys got in at the door.

"To see some friends."

"Who did you see?"

"Friends of mine," Gladys repeated.

"Of mine, too?" Mrs Sperber was on her guard.

"Oh yes, friends of yours, too."

"Who were they?"

"You wouldn't remember them."

Mrs Sperber was exasperated. "I suppose you told them a nice tale about your mother."

"They knew already," said Gladys.

"Where have you been?" Mrs Sperber almost screamed at her.

"To the cemetery."

Mrs Sperber did not quite know how to take this information. On the one hand she was moved by it and felt very tender towards Gladys. On the other, she was slightly suspicious. "Did you go for a rehearsal?" she whispered.

Gladys could not answer. She wondered why people knew so much and guessed so much and understood so very little.

"There's time, there's time," her mother said.

"Mama," Gladys muttered, "I'm sorry about that bed. I'll get it up from the cellar."

Mrs Sperber began to cry and Gladys too, and they moved together and cried out their wilful misunderstandings in a flood of love and hatred, both so acute and equal that they harmonized and were supportable.

"Shall I make some tea?" Gladys suggested.

"I'll make it. You sit down and rest." Mrs Sperber went into the scullery.

Gladys shuddered in her coat. She felt she had to come to a decision. But why or what about, she did not know. If only something would *happen*, she thought, to present a choice one way or the other. If the telephone would ring and some stranger were to ask her to marry him, or if the house burnt down with everything in it, except her and her mother. Or if there were a war or an epidemic or a good fairy to grant you three wishes, or anything at all that would slow the rhythm of the grandfather clock or interrupt the making of the tea. She picked up the newspaper and read her horoscope. "The day is uneventful but the evening is full of romance," it promised. With a desperate faith to believe in something, Gladys took off her coat and felt a lot better. "I'll get the tea, Mama," she called out. Their politeness towards one another was becoming embarrassing to both. Soon it would break and to-day would become like yesterday and all their to-morrows.

"I found your rent money," Mrs Sperber said as they sat over their tea.

"So you owe me an apology."

"But I can't for the life of me remember signing the book," Mrs Sperber insisted.

"But where else could the money have come from? It must be my rent."

"I've got other money," Mrs Sperber said proudly. "You're not my only source of income. Thank God, I've enough of my own. I don't have to depend on anybody."

"Well, d'you admit I paid you the rent or not?"

"How am I to know? The money's there all right, but it might have come from anywhere and anyway I don't remember signing."

Gladys did not feel like going out again. It was best to say no more about the matter. The evening held promise of romance. And so the rest of the day passed inevitably until Mrs Sperber declared she was tired and therefore they both had to go to bed.

"I'm not tired," Gladys said. "You go up on your own. I'm going to read a little." The evening was not yet over. There was still a chance.

"All right," said Mrs Sperber, "I'll read too." She sat yawning over the newspaper, with one eye on Gladys' book, looking for the end of the chapter. When it came in sight, she gave Gladys time to reach it, and then suggested retiring once more. "You're not going to finish that book to-night, are you?" she asked, when Gladys showed no signs of stopping.

"You don't have to wait for me," Gladys said between the lines. "I'll turn all the lights off."

Mrs Sperber settled down to her paper once more. The evening dragged itself out until Gladys decided it had had its chance. She closed the book. Her mother had fallen asleep in her chair, and the newspaper lay in her lap. Gladys picked it up and read the horoscope once more. Then she noticed that the paper was a week old, and since every day had been the same she knew that it could never have been true. But perhaps to-morrow.

"I'm ready," she said. "I'm going to bed."

Mrs Sperber started from her sleep. "I must have fallen off," she laughed and gathered her bag from behind her, checked its contents and followed Gladys upstairs.

Gladys was first in bed, propped up on her own and what had been Sid's pillow, and, because she knew that she hated it, she watched her mother undress. Mrs Sperber did not even let herself watch herself undressing, and placed herself in a part of the room where there was no reflection from the many mirrors either for herself or for Gladys. It took her a little time to find such a position, because the slant of the dressing-table mirror was never the same every night. Before beginning the operation, she closed her eyes and kept them closed, like a child, who on shutting his own eyes, believes he is invisible. She kept her dress on to the very last, and fiddled underneath it like a shy bather undressing on an open beach. The first garment to emerge after long and intricate fiddling was the corset, which she

217

spread out on the bed. The yards of criss-cross pink tape fell in two loose ends on either side and the suspenders attached curled on the counterpane like four sinners newly hanged. The stockings were next. They had already concertinaed down to her calves and, supporting herself on the bed-rail, she took them off one by one, and laid them in the rounded bowl of the corset. After intervals of more fiddling, when Mrs Sperber looked as if she were knitting a complicated pattern underneath her dress, and all the time with her eyes firmly shut, more and more articles of underwear emerged and were dropped into the corset as Mrs Sperber grew thinner and thinner. She lifted her dress gingerly and wriggled out of the arms, but kept the dress draped from her neck like a tent. In this way she was able to rid herself of all her underclothing and all that remained was the top garment.

But before taking the final step, she felt for all the things she had taken off, checking them one by one, and then rolled them slowly into the corset, tying up the bundle securely with one of the end tapes. This roll she placed gently inside the bed alongside where she would sleep, like a teddy-bear. Her bag she placed under the pillow and, at the same time, she withdrew a night-dress, which she placed handily on the bed, so that the interval between taking off her dress and putting on the nightgown would not be too long. She was now ready for the last move. Criss-crossing her arms, she drew her dress over her neck and let it fall to the floor, and, as she groped for her nightdress, Gladys looked at her.

Her body was like a filleted kipper that had been

oversmoked and dried. Her stomach hung like an un-pressed curtain reaching down to her thighs on which the strains of her child-bearing were chalked up in mother-of-pearl. Her feet were tiny and had often had to bear the weight of her children, so that the body had leaned forward to balance the burden. And now, even though the emaciated body presented no problem of balance, it still from custom leaned forward like the stubborn mast-head of a storm-tossed ship. What had once been breasts had shrunk into two cavities, the nipples, flag-poles of remembrance. Over it all she threw the nightgown transparent and blue, and the lace-filled puffed sleeves deflated on her wilted arms. She felt around for the bedclothes and crawled inside, cradling the corset on one arm. She opened her eyes and caught Gladys watching her.

"You can turn the light off now," she said angrily. "I'm ready."

When the room was dark, Mrs Sperber's anger burnt inside her.

"You owe me three months' rent," she started again.

"I paid you. You know I paid you. You told me you had the money."

"That's not your rent money. That's from something else."

"It's not true," Gladys shouted at her. "You know it's mine."

"May the Almighty strike me dead if I'm telling a lie."

And for once, He took up her challenge.

5 Gladys woke in the morning and got up immediately. She dressed and went downstairs to prepare her mother's tea. The newspaper lay with a few letters on the hall floor. She picked it up and turned immediately to the horoscope. "You may easily offend a close relation," it warned. "To-day is a day for keeping your temper." That could be true for any day, Gladys thought disappointedly. There was no sound from the bedroom upstairs, so she dallied over the paper. The forecasts for other people were more inventive. Leos were to have a surprise and Capricorns a financial setback. It's all a lot of rubbish, she thought, and read her own once more. Then she folded the paper and put it on the tray to take upstairs. The bedroom door was as she had left it, half open, her own bed scarcely disturbed and the heap of her mother on the other side.

"It's nine o'clock," she announced. "I've brought your tea."

She put the tray down on the safe and shook her mother by the shoulder. The sheet covered her chin and she lay very peacefully. "Mama," Gladys said again, "your tea." There was no answer. Gladys was afraid. "I don't see why I should get up and make you tea if you don't want it," she shouted at her. "I'll leave it. Don't let it get cold."

Gladys moved quickly away from the bed. She knew that something had happened. Something had interrupted the monotony of her life, that the tea was left to get cold and maybe the clock had stopped down-

220

stairs. But she did not want to know. She suddenly wanted nothing to happen. Nothing. She felt a guilt creeping on her and she rushed back to the bed and pulled the sheet off her mother's face.

Mrs Sperber lay like a child, still cradling the rolled corset on her arm. Her wrinkled face looked like a mask of corrugated silk. The little salt-bag had burst round her neck, the salt had trickled into a mound on the sheet, as if a life-full of tears had, at its end, become solid. Gladys bent down to kiss her. "God rest your soul," she said.

The family arrived soon afterwards. A long life was mutually wished all round, and Gladys felt it as a curse. She had a good life, they all insisted. It had to come. She'd had more than her years, and what better way to die? When they had all endowed their mother with the advantages she had reaped from life, they all felt a lot better. Nobody mentioned the sudden freedom that they all felt and each marvelled at the fact that such a weak old woman had been such a strong fetter on their lives. But Gladys felt no freedom, only a sharp and painful tightening of the chain. She saw no marvels in her mother's life or great happiness. Only misery and self-pity and many unwanted years. Unconsciously, she fingered the lapel of her dressing-gown and rubbed the cloth between her fingers. She looked at the faces of her family and wondered who could be called the chief mourner or mourner at all.

"The Lord giveth and the Lord taketh away," Mottel began and made his way up the stairs. The others followed him, and Gladys remained alone, staring at the outworn horoscope that still lay on the table and wondering whether this was what was meant by a promise of romance.

And when Emma Sperber was decently buried in the earth and the safe indecently broken open and the estate shared out, Gladys found herself in possession of the house and the larger share of her mother's valuables. The house was empty now, and Gladys alone, as she had so often wished. And the tea was there and the clock and the crumbs on the table: the wall of certificates, the dining-room table and the three dolls on the sofa. It was all there. And every night she would sit on her mother's bed and curse her for not being in it, and every week for the rest of her life she visited the cemetery and built a pyramid of pebbles on her mother's grave.

THE WHITE CUTTER

David Pownall

In the thirteenth century, an age half-crazed in its quest for certainty, King Henry seeks solace in the building of cathedrals. But Christians do not make good architects. To create the illusion of permanence – those soaring wonders in stone – Henry knows to rely on the masons, the secret brotherhood whose very craft disguises a dangerous heresy and creates a blasphemous beauty.

The White Cutter is the confession of Hedric, son of an itinerant stonemason, reared in a tool-bag, who becomes the greatest architect of his age. It tells of rumbustious adventures; of his sexual apprenticeship; of his unique education; of rogue clerics, singular nuns and The Four, a secret cabal teetering on the brink of genius and dementia.

It is a book which reveals much about light and stone, God and the Devil, father and sons, the Church and the State, love and murder, our need for secrecy and our need for uncontradicted truth in an age of chaos.

0 349 10117 5
ABACUS FICTION

Bernice Rubens

☐ MATE IN THREE	£4.99
☐ BROTHERS	£5.99
☐ MR WAKEFIELD'S CRUSADE	£4.99
☐ OUR FATHER	£4.99
☐ BIRDS OF PASSAGE	£4.99
☐ SUNDAY BEST	£4.99
☐ PONSONBY POST	£4.99
☐ ELECTED MEMBER	£4.99
☐ SPRING SONATA	£4.99
☐ FIVE YEAR SENTENCE	£4.99
☐ MADAME SOUSATZKA	£4.99

Abacus now offers an exciting range of quality titles by both established and new authors. All of the books in this series are available from:
Sphere Books, Cash Sales Department,
P.O. Box 11, Falmouth, Cornwall TR10 9EN.

Alternatively you may fax your order to the above address. Fax No. 0326 76423.

Payments can be made as follows: Cheque, postal order (payable to Macdonald & Co (Publishers) Ltd) or by credit cards, Visa/Access. Do not send cash or currency. UK customers: please send a cheque or postal order (no currency) and allow 80p for postage and packing for the first book plus 20p for each additional book up to a maximum charge of £2.00.

B.F.P.O. customers please allow 80p for the first book plus 20p for each additional book.

Overseas customers including Ireland, please allow £1.50 for postage and packing for the first book, £1.00 for the second book, and 30p for each additional book.

NAME (Block Letters) ....

ADDRESS..

....

☐ I enclose my remittance for_____

☐ I wish to pay by Access/Visa Card

Number ☐☐☐☐☐☐☐☐☐☐☐☐☐☐☐☐

Card Expiry Date ☐☐☐☐